Aurora and the Monster

STANDALONE MONSTER ROMANCE

SOPHIA SMUT

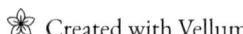

Chapter One

 urora

Scores of voices surrounded me like an uncomfortable embrace. I tried to open my eyes but my lids were heavy and the rest of me ached with a dull pain.

Somewhere near, loud pants carried to me on the wings of a hot breath and a huge presence loomed, casting darker shadows over me. Whoever it was smelled earthy and fresh.

Then, a touch, slimy and unpleasant. Full panic gripped my body while I struggled to wake up and react. Movement was impossible and everything hurt like hell. How long had I been asleep?

"Leave us now. Protect the door and let me take care of this little beauty," a rough, booming voice roared, sending a shiver down my spine.

Once more I tried to move and at last, I was able to raise my arms. My skin tingled with awareness. Someone, *something* foul was taking over my space and I needed to get up and run as far as my legs would take me...

Disoriented, my mind foggy, I attempted to take a few deep breaths. It was time for me to wake from this cruel dream.

"I should pierce your heart with a blade and end your life, little beauty, but the light inside me brightens when I look at you."

My heart pounded in my chest as I waited for my end, for there was no mistaking the meaning in his words. I didn't want to die like this, before I could inhale fresh air and see the world once again, before I returned to smelling the roses on the castle grounds and go riding with Phillip, my beloved prince.

I fought to open my eyes so I could see the beast or man or whatever it was that stood in front of me, but the curse set upon me was keeping me chained to my state.

Just then, he pressed his lips to mine and I froze

again. I tasted him, along with all the strength and passion that flowed from his body to mine.

Deep down I wanted to scream with rage, but he was suddenly devouring my lips, inhaling my scent, drawing out my soul—his energy connecting with mine.

Scorching heat rushed through my body, igniting my core, and my toes curled. How was this possible? The feeling was intense, arousing, and scandalous because I had no knowledge of this man who was devouring me. He was a stranger, a random visitor doing something that had been denied me for decades. Forbidden by a cruel fate.

When he finally stopped, I released a breath and at last, my eyelids fluttered, as if something about that kiss broke the last of the resistance within me that had kept me trapped in the darkness for so long.

At first, the whole world around me was barely visible in blurred tones. I moved my hands as I regained sensation in my limbs. The warmth I'd just felt on my lips suddenly moved down my chest, then my stomach and farther down to my core, making me gasp. I was not cold and numb anymore, but sentient, with heat flowing through me.

The image of my surroundings sharpened as my vision improved. I recognised everything—my chamber and my bed—but my memories were still very raw. I didn't even remember how I got here in the first place. My breaths were irregular and heavy, and my nightgown was stuck to my back.

"And she's awakened. That's a surprise," the same loud, rough voice spoke again and my head snapped instinctively to my right.

A giant of a man stood close, so close, staring down at me. He was bare-chested, muscular, and beautiful. Shock filled me at the sight, and my eyes felt like they were about to pop out of their sockets. His leather pants hung low on his hips, revealing a smattering of dark hairs on his torso. He was blond, his hair unkempt and long, but it was his eyes that drew me instantly to this stunning creature.

Fear washed over me like a tidal wave because I was certain that this man wasn't a normal human. Indeed, he looked like a mutant ... some kind of beast. His purple eyes regarded me with purpose as if he was looking into my very soul. Flustered, I shook my head.

"What ... who are you? Where is Phillip? And my father ... the king?" I asked weakly, not recognising my own voice. My throat felt raw and sore. I wanted to remember so many details but my memories faded in and out.

I shuddered when he kept looking at me as though ready to consume me.

He smirked, tilting his head to the side. His gaze moved down to my lips, then my cleavage. I took a sharp inhale, feeling so exposed. He was bigger than any man I had ever seen. His muscular chest was enormous and a random thought hit me where I wondered how it would feel if he held me close. I wanted to touch my lips, as if that would help me confirm whether he'd been the one who kissed me and awakened me from my deep sleep.

"They are all dead. My men have killed everyone in the castle. Now it's just you and me, my Princess Aurora," he said, standing to his feet and looking impossibly large and menacing.

Dead. A whimper escaped me, but I couldn't summon an ounce of grief. I was empty, drained, a shell without a past.

Once more I couldn't move, either because my muscles were stiff or because I was too afraid for my life. I could feel every ounce of this giant creature's power and more than anything, inexplicably, I wanted to be touched by his enormous arms and hands. Perhaps this scared me the most.

Despite the handsome face though, shadows of pain crept over his expression. What was his story and why was he here? Why was everyone dead? I couldn't even remember who those people were. My parents—I *knew* they'd existed yet not much of my life with them.

I shook my head in puzzlement. Or perhaps I simply didn't want his words to sink in. "No, you're lying to me. Phillip was here. He was the one who woke me up!" I shouted, remembering that other moment from the past.

Prince Phillip. I knew him—Phillip was safe ... familiar. I also knew who I was and I vaguely assumed the king and queen would probably be worried about me. Tears forced their way to my eyes, but I blinked to stop them from falling. I wasn't going to cry in front of this ... this brute. I didn't want to give him the satisfaction.

"Oh, princess, it seems you believe in fairytales, but the truth is that I was the one who woke you up. I came here to end your life, but instead I tasted your lips. I felt your arousal for me," he said, leaning closer and making me shiver.

Then, I caught movement at the periphery of my vision. A limb or something long and strange started to grow out of his body. At first I thought it could be a tail or another arm, but this would have been impossible. Then another one emerged, and another. Several tentacles came into view, appearing out of nowhere, sprouting from his flesh and gliding gracefully up and down like gentle waves.

I screamed in terror. "What are you? Stay away from me!" I shouted when one of the tentacles caressed my cheek, its texture wet and slimy. I pulled back in disgust but the beast laughed. I needed to run but my body refused to obey me and let me escape.

At least four tentacles had grown from each side, swirling like snakes in the air. I couldn't speak or breathe because then it occurred to me that this thing —this monster—had just kissed me.

"You ... you're ... don't touch me!" I shrieked.

"My name is Baadar and I'm your new king, little one. Stop lying to me. You were aroused by that kiss. I could read your emotions like an open book," he hissed as one of his tentacles caressed my arm.

Still I wanted to get away from him, but my body kept failing me.

I frantically looked around, trying to figure out what to do. Was he really going to kill me?

"Never! You disgust me and you're never going to be my king!" My voice was scratchy, rising in pitch and breaking at the end.

I thrashed around on the bed as he held me captive, relieved I could at least do that, and the movement made my breasts bounce. His gaze roved over my body,

9

pausing to take in my hardened nipples. I guessed my body didn't agree with my actions, even though I wouldn't ever admit it. I couldn't be all hot and bothered by this monster. This was insanity at best.

All of this had to be a product of my imagination. But then why did I feel so alive when his tentacles caressed my arm? When he'd kissed me before? I panted as he stared at me with a hunger and thirst for all that was forbidden.

Then, one of his tentacles shot outward and wrapped itself around my waist. My gown was so thin and I only just then realized I was wearing nothing underneath. I couldn't even remember why or if my maid had helped me change or whether I'd dressed myself.

"Don't lie to me, human. I haven't decided yet what I am going to do with you but look how wet you are for your master. Your scent is driving me mad and I'm thirsty for your blood, too," he growled, his huge tentacles lifting me off the bed and slamming me against the wall.

The impact drew a scream of pain from me. This was it. Soon, I'd be taking my last breath. Phillip was never going to rescue me from this monster because he was dead.

His piercing purple eyes bore into mine as he

approached me. I smelled the earthiness of his flesh that reminded me of balmy summer nights. I lost all sense of time as his huge body crashed into mine, violently and possessively. His hard muscles pressed against me while his beautiful mouth was only inches from mine.

I wanted to turn my head and look away but found myself unable to, rooted to the spot as I was, mesmerized by his eyes.

Then, something hard and big poked me between my legs.

"So beautiful ... and you smell divine when you're scared, my princess. It would be such a shame to slit your throat just now." He leaned closer and sniffed me, then reached out to move a stray lock of hair away from my flustered face. As much as I tried to stop it, scorching heat rushed through me and desire muddled my head. I hated feeling this way for a vile creature like this.

But all thought was sucked away from my brain when a ridged, yet oddly smooth, wet tentacle moved over my backside, then slid right between my legs.

"For the love of—" I wheezed, my words stopping because I couldn't speak. When the thing brushed over my sex, I wanted to yell out my pleasure and it took everything I had in me to hold that back. My body trembled, out of control, radiating with energy. I bit my bottom lip, once more tamping down a cry of ecstasy.

"You won't deceive me, princess," he muttered. "Just one more kiss. One more, before I kill you."

And then he pressed his lips to mine in a mind-blowing, explosive and urgent kiss while his tentacle rubbed itself over my clit. I moaned into his mouth as this was all too much. The pressure between my legs was unbearable and his lips tasted like ambrosia, earth and sun.

He kissed me like the monster he was, as though he'd never tasted a human woman before––yearning and desperate. My body made all the decisions as I opened up to him, parting my lips and allowing his tongue to caress mine. His mouth was suddenly every-where, hard and demanding.

This was better than the first time and I was soaked for him. My juices gushed down my leg as his probing tentacle continued to violate me.

"Tell me, my princess, do you want me to touch you down there and lick your precious cum off your thigh?" he asked, ending the kiss. He, too, seemed to struggle with his breathing.

His tentacle retracted and I was suddenly disappointed it wasn't touching me anymore. I must have lost my mind.

My chest rose and fell in rapid movements as I stared at him, hardly believing my eyes as I tried to gather my wits, tried to understand ... how could I want more?

"Let me go. I hate you," I spat, and he smirked in reaction.

Kneeling in front of me, he forced my legs apart.

"Wrong answer," he murmured before everything went dark again.

Chapter Two

Baadar

I stood in front of the cage in which the princess now resided, staring at her through the bars. She was so fucking gorgeous with her flaxen hair and sparkling green eyes I could drown in. My cock was still hard for her. The memory of her moaning into my mouth remained fresh in my mind. I had to quell an urge to squeeze her throat while my tentacle caressed her clit. There was no way I could have controlled myself, so I pulled away and put a spell on her, so she'd return to her slumber.

She'd claimed she didn't want me to touch her, but

that was a lie. Her body spoke a language I was able to understand.

Since the day I was forced to live with the curse, I gained the ability to easily sniff out the emotions of humans. She could deny it all she wanted, but Aurora desired me with a ferocity that terrified her. If her soul could talk, she'd beg me to fill every orifice on her body with my cock and tentacles.

I could see the fear in her eyes when I showed her my true nature, but at the same time, her body trembled with need for me. The sweet scent of her arousal addled my brain, triggering the beast within me. I longed to consume her, to make her mine in every way possible.

This put a damper on my plans. I arrived at the castle ready to put an end to the soul responsible for this damned curse by slaying everyone inside it—including her. Why did she have to taste like honey and lilies?

I had never felt this way before. I had always taken what I wanted, including the life of many humans. She had to be rotten like her father and the rest of her family. But instead of doing what I set out to do, I made her my captive.

I felt a pull toward the princess that I couldn't explain. I wanted to protect her, to keep her safe from harm. But at the same time, I had to claim her, to make her mine in every possible fucking way. Her body was my possession to play with.

Yet, I couldn't have both. I couldn't own her and get my revenge. The thought of having to choose filled me with rage and frustration. The monster inside me struggled to take control and simply claim what it saw as its own. But I also felt a new emotion, one unfamiliar to me: compassion. Beast and man engaged in a battle for dominance—a war that might either save me or kill me.

I sat down in front of the cage, resting my head on my hand. Closing my eyes, I tried to make sense of the turmoil inside me. The sound of Aurora's soft breaths filled the space, and even that stirred the inner beast.

If the tentacles were out, I'd be suffering even more because right now, no other woman would do. My body knew before the rest of me did. I would claim her, fill her with my seed, own her body and soul. Yet, this posed a real danger and I didn't want to hurt her.

I was no man, but a beast in every sense of the word. An abomination.

The world feared me. Despised me.

I opened my eyes and rested them on her again. I couldn't keep her locked up here forever. I needed to make a decision.

Let her go? Or claim her as mine?

Either way, my life would never be the same again because she was still living and breathing. Those who'd turned me into a monster had to pay for their sins. They needed to perish—and she was one of them.

I stood to my feet and walked away, my mind in turmoil and my body on fire for her.

I'd fucked many women in the past, peasants and women of stature and others in between, but copulating with me had a price. Many did not survive the experience and therefore, they were unable to satisfy me. Aurora was different, I could sense that.

I needed time to think, to figure out if her death could free me from the chains that had enslaved me for so long. Any decision I made might impact the lives of many. My army, those who'd remained loyal to me ...

The king and queen had escaped because they were fucking cowards. I'd lied to her earlier when I told her I'd killed them all. Fact was that my mission had failed.

I walked out of the cave, thinking about my princess and pondering the many methods I'd use to break her. This would take some time, but I was ready for anything. First though, I needed to speak with my men about the captured prince. I had ordered them to bring him back to me, but I had not yet had a chance to question him. I needed to know how and why he'd ended up in the forest with the witch.

Witches were a rarity. Most had been killed by dragons, but their magic was powerful and I had been searching for one since the day I'd been cursed. Prince Phillip would have the answers I was looking for.

As I walked, I could hear the muted murmurs of my men. They were all probably wondering why I hadn't killed Aurora yet. Also why I'd let her get under my skin. They were gathered around a large fire, cooking a deer they had caught earlier. I could smell the delicious scent of roasting meat and it made my stomach growl.

"My lord," Gerald, one of the men, said, bowing his head as I approached. "Prince Phillip is being held in the cells, as you ordered."

I nodded, feeling a sense of satisfaction. "Excellent. I hope he's in good enough shape to talk," I said. "I will question him myself right away."

"Yes, my lord."

"What about the witch? Wasn't she with him?" I asked.

"She vanished the moment we apprehended him," Gerald replied.

I walked toward the cells, annoyed that the witch had gotten away once again. The only one who might be able to undo the fucking curse Aurora's father was responsible for. Because I knew he'd hired her to do it.

If such was the case, I should proceed with my plan to kill the woman who made my cock stand at attention with a mere sigh. No heirs or relatives of the king ought to survive my vengeance.

I couldn't shake the feeling that there was something off about the prince and the witch being caught together in the forest. Why had he been alone with her in the first place? My gut told me they'd been engaging in some kind of dark magic, and I needed to get to the bottom of it.

When I arrived at the cell, I spotted the prince huddled in a corner, his eyes wide with terror and several strands of blond hair covering his eyes. I didn't expect him to be so handsome. Square jaw and bright blue eyes—I could see through the dirt on his face why Aurora would find him appealing, but this only angered me more.

Heat rose in the pit of my stomach as I studied him. Aurora had hoped he would be the one to break her sleeping curse. However, there'd been rumors in the kingdom that Phillip had never cared for her and he'd been planning to use her to steal the crown from his brother.

"Why were you in the forest with the witch?" I

growled, my voice low and menacing. No use in beating about the bush. "And where is she now? I need to find her!"

The prince hesitated, then rose and cleared his throat. "The witch has cast a spell on me," he finally said. "I found myself unable to resist her. She vanished the moment we were surrounded."

I wasn't fully convinced he was telling me the truth. Sure, the witch was powerful, but I didn't believe she could have enticed a man like him so easily by using her spells. She'd have more likely struck fear in him first.

"What were you doing with her?" I asked again, tilting my head to the side and fixing him with an intense stare. My cock twitched then and my tentacles started to break through the surface of my skin. This was strange in every way. I wasn't attracted to this man in front of me but my anger and the urgency of the situation were playing games with me.

The prince's eyes stayed on me. I could see he was trying to figure out if it was worth it for him to talk to me.

"I ... I am not sure I should say..." he muttered, his voice rising a little at the end.

"Speak, or I shall cut your tongue out and feed it to

the pigs," I warned in a tone that would have made Attila the Hun shit in his goat-hide pants.

He swallowed, and was that a yelp that just escaped his lips? Fucking coward, like the rest of them.

"Speak! Now!" I ordered, so loud the words bounced off the walls in the cavernous space.

He jumped and raked a hand through his hair.

"And don't even think of feeding me a lie. I can tell if you are and then, I'd have to torture you for a lot longer."

He nodded, swallowing again. "I ... I knew she liked unusual sexual activities so I sought her out. I asked her to pee on me and she gladly did it," he finally said.

The hint of a smirk showed on his face. Princely arrogance was hard to suppress—even in the face of a threat. He straightened to his full height of about six feet or so. A fucking dwarf creature, compared to me. "And I loved it. This kind of ... thing ... turns me on. The witch was thrilled, too. You know, man to man."

Okay. So we went from classy prince material to fucking pervert in a second flat. What would possess a man like this to admit to such crap? Yes, I was a beast and all, but hell...

"Not sure I do know, *Prince* Phillip," I said, my voice dripping with sarcasm.

This was the type of deranged thing he'd want Aurora to do with him.

More intense rage coursed through me, bowling through my common sense. Why would I even be jealous of this idiot? Yet here I was, pondering the many ways I could end his life, slowly and painfully.

The mysterious witch had urinated on him and he'd taken pleasure from it. Interesting and unexpected, to be sure. Even more so that he'd admit to such a proclivity this freely, despite the fact I'd hardly given him any choice.

"How did you even find her?" I growled. "They are all dead. I have been hunting for this one for centuries."

He smirked more visibly now, self-confidence making a show. He then rubbed his hand over his crotch. The heat from his stare made me shudder.

Creep.

"She joined me in the tavern where I was enjoying the company of a few ladies," he said in a low voice. "She told me she could help me save Aurora, to break the curse she was under. She asked me to follow her, so I did. Her porcelain skin and blue eyes drew me in. But then things took an unexpected turn. She stopped while we were going through the forest, pulled my pants down, and started sucking me off." He shook his head, his expression one of awe. "How could I refuse such a bold invitation?"

My cock enjoyed the story immensely, bringing my beastly nature to the fore. The image of the witch moving her mouth over Phillip's length was quite appealing, especially when the witch looked like Aurora and Phillip looked like me.

The more I fantasized, the more my cock grew.

And the more my cock grew, the more I wanted to fuck.

A beast I was, and a beast I'd likely always remain.

Men didn't normally interest me, but there were no women around and I had to slake my desire.

Either this or rush to Aurora and risk killing her with my violent needs because I wanted her too much.

Again, I couldn't hurt her.

A roar escaped me, and the bastard cowered. My tentacles wanted out. "Too bad I already broke your princess's curse. I went to the castle to end her, but instead I saved her, " I growled, wanting him to know she wasn't his to rescue.

This man obviously didn't have any feelings for Aurora. He needed her for his own ends. She was a commodity to him—nothing else. In my mind, he was entirely expendable.

What was *she* to me though? An object? A slave? I

had no idea, but the thought of this fool touching her in any way was completely unacceptable.

The prince had the decency to look shocked. "But I was supposed to get to her first!"

I approached the bars, forcing my tentacles to stay put as he stared at me.

"Maybe, but now she's mine and you're going to rot in here for a while unless you take me to the witch."

The prince laughed and dragged his hand nervously through his hair.

"She's gone." His voice trembled as he spoke—he wasn't as composed as he wanted me to believe. "Your men scared her away and she won't come back, so why don't you come inside the cell? I think we have a lot to discuss." He stared at me and I wondered how far his perversions went.

I leaned forward and inhaled his scent. Could I use this to my advantage?

Could I have him at my mercy, toy with him and his desires until he gave me what I wanted at last?

Chapter Three

Aurora

I woke up lost and confused. My whole body ached. It took me some time to figure out where I was. This cell with iron bars was damp and dark, there was one tiny window close to the ceiling that I couldn't reach, and the whole place smelled of death.

My body felt oddly numb and tingly in all the inappropriate places and apart from that, the lower part of my stomach was badly hurting. My head throbbed as though a hammer was bearing down on it, cracking it open.

My memories started to come back as I slowly got

up to stretch my limbs, like a slow moving cloud heading toward me from miles away. At last, I could see its shape, its cottony white hue.

I had been cursed. My father and mother were shouting at the old hag that stood in the main hall, throwing accusations at her. The hag glanced at me—her teeth were rotten and her face all wrinkled up. A disguise, for sure.

Then I remembered a blinding green light and nothing after that. This was probably the moment when she cast her spell on me.

After that, the memories from a few hours earlier rushed through me like a tornado, and I gasped.

"This had to be a dream. The monster that kissed me isn't real," I said to myself, feeling painful cramps in the lower part of my stomach. I started taking long, deep breaths when something wet and sticky slid between my legs. Luckily, the monster didn't chain me to the wall so I could move freely.

The cell itself had a musty smell that made me even more trapped and claustrophobic. Then I remembered his lips on mine and I shuddered.

"You didn't like it," I told myself in this place where only the walls could hear me. His tentacles were terrifying, slimy and off-putting, yet they brought out something wild and feral in me ...

Oh shit, what had the hag done to me? Did the curse remove my ability to make commonsense judgments on people and situations? And most importantly, honest-to-goodness beasts?

My body responded in ridiculous ways when he was close. My heart raced, my hands all sweaty. And no one had ever kissed me like that before. Including Phillip.

When Phillip's lips brushed over mine, I enjoyed it, but he never made me want to lose control like the man-creature with tentacles that had broken the hag's curse over me.

I must have been asleep for a very long time. Baadar claimed that he'd killed everyone, my entire family, but was this really the truth?

I took a few long, deep breaths, and then I reached out to slide my hand between my legs. I touched myself then examined my bloodied fingers, thinking there couldn't have been a worse moment to get my period. When I got up, I heard some noise in the distance. Someone was approaching. Suddenly, the door to my cell creaked open and two men appeared at the threshold.

"The master wants to see you, princess," one of them said, walking inside.

I wiped the blood over my dress because I had

nowhere to clean my hands, then stood on my feet, a little unsteadily.

"Whoa," I whispered, holding on to the bed for a moment. Soon, I found my bearings and my head cleared a little. My body was stiff and achy, but I felt better. Sure, my dress was dirty and I desperately needed a bath—wishful thinking, for sure.

"Fine, just take me to him," I said, my tone firm. I might have no clue what to expect, but I was still Princess Aurora and I'd go through this hell with my head high.

They led me through what I can only describe as a dark, nasty dungeon. A few cells were occupied, others empty. The overwhelming odor of blood, sweat, and death made me nauseous, but I told myself I had to be strong.

My stomach was still cramping, my blood rolling down my legs. *Ugh!* The monster would probably smell it on me, and this was going to be embarrassing. I wasn't sure if he planned to kill me or let me go, because I couldn't imagine staying here, captive to him.

I needed to take care of this unfortunate situation —but if death awaited me, should I care about menstruating and cleaning myself up?

As we turned a corner, I spotted a figure in one of the cells. The man struck me as familiar, bearing a resemblance to someone I knew ... oh yes, he did! I stopped and grabbed the bars as hope flickered through me.

"Phillip? Phillip, is that you?" I shouted. The man lifted his head and then I recognized his green eyes. He looked terrible, but I knew this was my prince.

"Aurora?" he asked in astonishment.

The guards were giving me impatient looks, but I wasn't going to move. I needed only a few moments to figure out if this was indeed my Prince Phillip. I reached out through the bars, touching him when he crawled closer.

"Yes, it's me, but what are you doing here? Have you been caught by the monster?" I asked.

"I can't believe you're awake, Aurora, after all these years! Baadar told me he woke you up from the curse, and I begged him to spare you."

"Hurry up, princess. The master doesn't like to be kept waiting," one of the guards barked, grabbing me and pushing me forward.

"Just stay strong. I'll get you out of here, I promise, so have faith," I told him, before I was dragged away from the cell. The guards were stronger and I didn't want them to touch me, so I carried on walking until we left the dungeon.

I was shocked and saddened by the sight of my

prince in such a state. Rage toward the monster grew, as well as my determination to save Phillip and myself from this predicament.

If Phillip was alive, how about other members of my family? I had to find out if anyone had survived and get us all out of here.

Finally, we emerged from the dungeon right to the outdoors. The forest spread out before us. As we walked, I thanked the universe for the balmy temperature—at least I didn't have to suffer through the cold. I tried to not think about the twigs and small pebbles cutting into my feet as we walked. I guessed it would be too much to ask for a pair of shoes.

The menstrual pain intensified with my anxiety, so I had to pause and bend down a few times, waiting for the pain to pass.

It seemed like an eternity had passed when an imposing dark tower came into view. One of the guards grabbed my arm and barked at me to keep moving.

I gasped, taking in the monstrous manor that now came into view. Moments later, I was shoved through the large giant doors and taken through several dark corridors. Men were stationed everywhere, all humans that reminded me of my father's guards.

"The master is waiting for you. Just go in through

that door," one of my captors said, pointing to an entrance ahead.

I nodded, took a deep breath, then pushed the door open, walking straight into a large chamber. Several oil lamps and torches brightened up the whole space, yet I still felt a chill seeping into my skin.

The monster stood by the window, dressed in a crisp red shirt and black pants, and surprisingly, from that angle, he actually looked civilized and noble. His tentacles were hidden away.

A vicious cramp tore at my lower stomach and I bent a little, wincing and pressing a palm against the affected area. Just then, he turned around abruptly, catching me in the act.

"What's wrong with you, princess? Are you in pain?" Baadar asked, approaching me.

My face flushed because I suddenly remembered the way he'd held me when I woke up, then his huge tentacle sliding up my thigh to my sex. Licking my lower lip, I tamped down my whirling emotions as he grabbed my arm and loomed over me. He consumed me with his presence, and his deep blue gaze pierced through me, sending my senses into overdrive.

"Nothing ... it's nothing," I mumbled, because there was no way I was going to tell him the truth.

More blood trickled down my leg and I held a

breath as he studied me. I wished he'd step back a bit, put some distance between us. Overwhelmed by the intensity of his stare, I swallowed hard. His full lips begged to be tasted, but the very thought should fill me with shame. He was supposed to be vile, but my body didn't care.

He frowned. "You're in pain. Tell me why, right now. Did any of my men hurt you?" he demanded and I laughed at that.

"I don't know why you'd ask me that. I thought you wanted me dead, anyway," I pointed out, trying my damnedest to ignore the heat radiating from his body. I finally managed to pull away from him and take a step back.

"Stop talking back to me, princess, and tell me why you are in pain." His frown deepened.

Fuck him—no way was I going to confess the embarrassing nature of my discomfort. I was supposed to hate him and yet, his tone left me weak.

Oh, hell. Why did it matter to hold back anyway?

"I woke up and started menstruating," I scoffed, finally spilling the beans. I looked away in shame, feeling as though I was in front of my parents, waiting for them to approve of my outfit. My mother had been raised in a super strict household and that judgmental attitude stuck with her.

Baadar placed his hand over my thighs, his eyes wide. No one should be that good-looking, but it was just a facade for the beast that lay under the surface.

"That's why your scent is so much more enticing now ... hmmm, interesting," he murmured, watching me suddenly like a hungry beast. "Come with me, princess."

He went to open the door.

"Where are you taking me?" I asked, but he didn't answer.

I followed through more long, dark corridors, passing people—humans—dressed as servants or guards. They all bowed when he walked by them. Then we climbed down a staircase that seemed to lead underground.

Baadar pushed open another door and my face was hit with a sweet-smelling cloud of steam. The scent of soaps and oils permeated the air. He walked in and I followed like an obedient lamb, taking it all in. My pulse quickened as I was filled with a strange sense of anticipation.

His stare was fire, a blaze that ravaged whatever good sense I clung to. My nipples hardened and I felt naked, exposed.

I glanced behind me, seeing that two servants were shutting the door. We stood in some sort of washroom with a large pool of water in the middle. The basin was filled with flowers and steam rose from it. The cozy space offered comfort and warmth.

"Why are we here?" I asked, confused.

I found it hard to believe this was where he tortured people. He had admitted earlier that he wanted to kill me, so maybe he planned to drown me in a nice-smelling, oversized tub?

He tilted his head to the side. "Take your dress off and immerse yourself in the water," he ordered. "I'll relieve your pain, my princess."

What in the world was he talking about? My face was flushed and sweat trickled down my back. The water beckoned me, screaming at me to wash away the blood that no doubt coated my thighs now in thin rivulets. I could ask for some kind of special pad or cloth but I didn't see any females here. I bet the present company would have no idea what to do if I requested something like that. Of course, it was just my luck that on top of everything else, my time of the month came just when I woke up from a hundred-year-old sleeping curse. The gods had a twisted sense of humor.

I took a step back. "No, I don't need your help. Just let me go," I hissed and then another intense cramp tore through me. It was all I could do to not moan in pain. The monster's face changed. He didn't look the least bit happy as he shook his head.

"See? You don't need to suffer. Now get in the water like a good little princess. I'll release my tentacle and you will sit on my face. The moment you orgasm, you won't feel any pain."

Chapter Four

Baadar

I was supposed to be indifferent to her beauty and intelligence, but I couldn't stand to see her in pain. She was so determined to pretend that everything was all right. Her strength shone through, as well as her energy. The long sleep did nothing to dampen her spirit, it seems.

Her body was curvy in all the right places, and I couldn't stop myself from imagining her on her knees, sucking on my cock, while my mating tentacle gave her the required attention. I inhaled sharply, seeing her jaw drop as she worked on making sense of my words.

She teemed with excitement—the fact she tried to hide the extent of it made her even more alluring. Already, I could read her so well. It was her time of the month, the reason why she had me salivating. She smelled divine and I didn't care about the blood. I had plenty of blood on my hands, anyway, albeit not the pleasant kind.

I had to taste her soon or I'd lose my mind.

This washroom was kept on the ready for me at all times. The two servants here were completely devoted to me, just as I was to them. They all knew the price they would have to pay if any of them spoke of what went on in this space. I trusted them, and that trust worked both ways.

"You're so very beautiful when you blush," I said, inching closer to her. "Can't wait to taste that rich nectar…"

I'd lain with many mortal women, from whom I learned this trick. If a man made a woman orgasm during her menstrual days, it would relieve her of any pain.

"You can't be serious! I'm bleeding heavily right now… this is too humiliating," she said, her mouth dropping open.

I want to see her on her knees, servicing me and my tentacles with those delicious lips…

I could teach her obedience and more because she needed to understand that she belonged to me.

I also wanted her to suffer for the sins of her father, but right now all I wanted to do was possess her.

Taking away all that ailed her would be the first step in owning her mind, heart, and soul.

"I have much innocent blood on my conscience, my dear princess, but trust me when I say that I can provide unlimited pleasure to a woman," I said proudly, my tentacles rearing to burst forth. I was so *hard* for her. "Get into that water before I rip your clothes off and take you as you are. It will be my pleasure to drink every drop of your blood and watch you break apart for me."

Her eyes widened in both shock and unexpected desire. Deny it she might, but I knew she wanted me to fuck her. Her blood-stained pussy pulsated with need. She longed to feel my tentacles again, my mouth on hers, my exploring hands and all the depraved things I could do to her ... although she'd never admit it.

I had half a mind to drag that rotten cream puff, Prince Phillip, here and make him watch me play with the woman he would have deceived for his own, twisted ends. The young prince wanted the kingdom for himself, but he wasn't going to get his wish. There were so many ways I could use this pawn to my advantage...

Aurora's hesitation was brief. I did not miss the longing in her eyes when she glanced at the water, which was filled with many regenerating potions and spells, created by one of my alchemists. She bit her bottom lip, then seemed to come to a decision when she shifted on her feet. With a sigh, she removed her dress.

She stood before me in all her naked glory, her gaze unflinching. Bold and magnificent.

I took her all in, staring at her full breasts, round hips, and bloodied thighs. Her crotch looked like a mouthwatering murder scene.

I couldn't take my eyes off her. My monster begged to be unleashed at any moment but I didn't want to scare her. The image of her sitting on my face, feeding me her nectar, was too much to bear. I quickly removed my clothes, then gestured for my servants to take the garments away and burn them. It was better this way—easier.

Aurora hurried to the water and immersed herself in it. My men kept their eyes averted, as I expected them to. Luckily, she didn't notice my erection just yet.

She moaned in pleasure as she spread her arms and

legs and drifted in the water. A sight to behold that made my cock come close to bursting.

And just like that, my beast broke free. My tentacles grew, spreading out fast, whirling all around me. This was my second nature, and I was used to my monster by now. The mating tentacle spilled a bit of pre-cum as I stared at her perky breasts. She finally noticed me and jumped in fright, probably not expecting me so close. Her arms flailed as she splashed around and panted heavily.

When the mating frenzy gripped me, I was at the point of no return. I opened my mouth, releasing my long tongue. My two longest tentacles snaked through the water as I walked farther in.

"You can't escape me, princess. You have unleashed my monster," I growled as my tentacle grabbed her waist and lifted her above the water. Soon enough, both of my long tentacles wrapped themselves around her thick thighs and brought her closer to me.

"Stop it! No! I need to wash up more," she hissed, her tone laced with trepidation.

Her body was trembling, which reduced my control to a mere thread. All I wanted to do was ram my cock into her pink pussy. What the hell was wrong with me, and why was I suddenly so obsessed with the woman I was supposed to kill?

"It's clean enough for me. Let me finish the job with my tongue, my love," I growled, opening my mouth and showing her what the curse had done to me. Then I moved my tentacles to spread her legs wide while she whimpered and squirmed, fighting me to no avail.

She was right—she was still bleeding, but I was too fucking lost in my own desire and need to care about little things like that.

"Oh, for God's sake," she protested when my tentacles brought her closer to my face. Her scent was making me lose whatever was left of my mind, as did the sight of her perfect, bloody, and throbbing pussy.

So I dove in, let out my tongue and started licking her. I buried my face in her crotch to feast on her delectable juiced. She trembled against me, then let out a keening moan as her body tensed more and more. I tasted all of her, from her clit all the way to her anus. She cried out when for a moment, I focused only on her clit. I sucked on it and she shook violently as though hit by a bolt of lightning.

The coppery scent of her blood drove my mating tentacle crazy, ready to ejaculate. I groaned as I continued to suck on her bundle of nerves.

"For God's sake, please... please don't stop!" she screamed as I continued to give as good as I had.

Pausing on the sucking, I stuck my long tongue into her hole while I rubbed on her clit with my fingers. She shook and became putty in my arms, but my two tentacles held her tight while the others splashed in the water.

And then, Aurora came for me. She released a scream that bounced against the walls and shattered into a thousand tiny voices, lost in harmonious ecstasy. She convulsed, over and over, arching her head back as I fucked her hard and fast with my tongue. Her breasts bounced to the rhythm of my thrusts until at last, she went numb.

She tasted like honeycomb and vanilla. Blood and life. Divine. I couldn't get enough of her incredible scent that was now imprinted on my skin.

I pulled away to catch my breath and give her a few seconds to adjust before diving in again. My long tongue was moving in and out of her tight hole, and soon she was coming again, spreading her juices all over my face.

I wanted to turn her around, ram my hard cock into her and use my mating tentacle for her ass, but then I remembered this whole thing was all about her. My flesh was on fire, and I had no choice but to spill my seed in the water because she'd worked me up so much.

She kept exploding all over my face, the multiple orgasms wracking her while I enjoyed feasting on her bloody pussy.

There was something about the princess that made me completely lose control.

"Please stop ... I can't take it anymore..." she begged, hanging on to my tentacles.

I withdrew my tongue and slowly lowered her to the water as she panted for air.

This woman had snuck under my skin in mere moments. Already I couldn't imagine being apart from her, and this confused me because it wasn't something I'd grown used to.

My monster retracted so I became myself once more—King Baadar, the human. Still, I was riddled with need for Princess Aurora. No matter what form I took, beast or man, my desire did not waver.

I held her in my arms as she drifted above the water, taking long, deep breaths. Her perky pink nipples stuck out as her chest moved up and down in a fast rhythm.

I wanted to hold her in my arms for as long as possible. To feel her softness, as well as her courage. Aurora was my little firecracker, like no female I'd ever met.

"I don't feel any pain anymore. The cramping stopped," she breathed out after a moment.

I smiled at her, pleased with the outcome. Now though now I needed to figure out my goal. My tentacle needed a mate sooner rather than later, but why her? What would it say about me if I spared her for my own selfish wants? Would I lose respect among my people?

I wasn't supposed to like any of it, but the obsession to consume her wasn't going away. Maybe I needed to do something drastic to push her away, to get her out of my mind and see her the way I was supposed to see her: as the enemy.

"I'm so glad to hear it, princess. I must leave you now, so continue to enjoy your bath," I said, feeling a sudden urge to get away from her. This was too dangerous and I had to go elsewhere to clear my head.

She stood in the water, her breasts exposed. We faced each other, naked.

"What? Leave? But I am sure you expect the same from me? I can take care of you," she said confidently, licking her lips.

My heart was pounding and I hated that. Hated how she made me *feel*. "I do have things to take care of," I insisted weakly.

Her face fell but I held my guilt at bay.

I needed to find another woman to satisfy me, but that thought made me sick. Aurora was all over me, around me, in me. No matter where I went, what I did, I'd smell her scent.

I was in so much fucking trouble already and I suspected there was no way out of this.

Her offer was tempting for sure and I was ready to take her, but something held me back. Nobody could have this much power over me.

She reached out to grasp my hands with small fingers, but I pushed through the water and quickly got out.

"My servants will take care of your every need. Until the next time, Princess," I said, never turning to look at her face.

Then, I marched out of the room before she could say something that would hold me captive to her until the very end of my life.

Chapter Five

urora

After Baadar vanished, I stayed in the pool for a while, keeping one wary eye trained on his servants, who never left the room.

Shock clung to me like a thin veil of sweat oozing from my pores. My body wouldn't stop trembling. This beast, this enigma, had brought me pleasure I'd never felt before. And so fast, too—it took seconds for me to explode, and all while I was menstruating.

I couldn't decide what to make of that. It was humiliating at first, but then that changed into some-thing so ... erotic. Baadar hadn't minded at all that I was bleeding. The way he held me, showered me with attention, transported me to another realm—beyond this surreal mountain kingdom I had yet to make sense of. I had never experienced anything like it before and after he was gone, I wanted more.

My cramps were gone and although my period wasn't gone, I felt so much better. He had a magical touch—a dangerous thing. I kept telling myself I couldn't trust him. This monster had come to kill me and yet, I let him touch me in the most intimate of ways. True, I'd caught glimpses of vulnerability in him, but he hit it all too well.

I'd only just woken up into this world after an extended sleep, so I couldn't afford to let my guard down. I needed to figure out what had happened to my parents and my kingdom.

As I mulled different possibilities, the servants quietly exited the room. I couldn't believe I'd allowed Baadar to devour me with them present. Mortification came once more to the fore, so I hoped I wouldn't have to see them again any time soon.

Shortly after, two women entered the washroom, carrying what looked like new attire and towels.

"We are here to take you to your chamber, Princess," the blond one said, smiling at me. They were both beautiful and young. I suspected they had no magic in them, so I assumed they were ordinary human women who worked for Baadar. "We have cotton balls and pads for your monthly bleed, my lady, so you don't have to worry about anything. The master asked us to serve you the best way we can."

They handed me a towel when I came out of the pool and I quickly wrapped it around me. I glanced at the pile of clothes that the one with the darker skin was holding. This was all too much.

This morning I woke up in a dank, filthy cell, and now this. Warmth spread through my chest and I wanted to cry.

Baadar was obviously more humane than he cared to admit and I needed to find a way to gain his trust. My priority was to locate my family and regain our status on Mount Moorhead. Until I was cursed, I was next in line to be the Queen.

The curse wasn't gone yet. I could feel it deep within me. Therefore, I had to track the witch who had used black magic against me. She was the only one who could completely remove the curse. Still, I still had no idea why any of this had happened in the first place.

"Thank you so much," I replied, taking the clothes and changing into them.

They helped me dress, too, which was both familiar and endearing.

"Now we have to take you to your chamber. The master has requested that you rest before dinner," the blond one said as she assisted me in putting on the beautiful crimson dress with a low cleavage. After everything I'd been through, this felt like heaven. I did indeed feel like a princess and not the prisoner I truly was.

Thankfully, the pad they provided was effective in stopping me from bleeding all over my legs and I felt so relieved the monster had thought about everything for my comfort. He obviously wasn't going to throw me back in the cell, but I still had to figure out how to get my beloved Phillip out of there.

"Tell me more about Master Baadar. Has he been living here long? Has he got a consort?" I asked as we finally left the washroom and climbed to the floor above.

The two women told me they'd worked for Baadar for years and I knew this was my best opportunity to learn more about him. He obviously made a decision that he wasn't going to kill me. It seemed he was planning to keep me here, but for how long and why?

There was definitely a strong attraction between us that I attempted to conceal. He must have sensed it too and that was the main reason why was so attentive. Our first kiss kept playing on my mind and igniting little fires within me. For now, I was planning to push all my emotions aside because there were things that needed to be done.

Bianka, the darker one, who seemed more talkative, giggled in a girlish manner.

"No, the master often said that he's never going to have a consort—not until he finds the witch that can remove his monster curse," she explained.

The blonde, Mara, gave her a sharp look, but Bianka didn't seem phased. She looked like she wanted to tell me more.

"Curse?" I asked straight away. "I have seen his real nature and your master can indeed be terrifying."

"I don't think we should talk to you about Master Baadar, Princess. People like to talk and we don't want to get into trouble," Mara quickly added, lowering her voice.

"It's only us so don't worry, I won't say anything to anyone. Did you know I have been victim of a sleeping curse for years, too?"

They both widened their eyes in shock as we entered what they told me was to be my chamber.

"So you're the sleeping princess from the Mount Moorhead kingdom?" Mara asked.

I nodded.

"Yes, so can you imagine what that was like, sleeping for so long. I don't even know what happened to my parents and the rest of the kingdom. I know that your master captured my prince," I continued, hoping they would feel bad enough for me and tell me everything.

"The master was cursed into becoming a tentacle monster a long time ago–some say over a hundred and fifty years ago–by Crystalia, the witch from the Seven Mountains. It was his brother that made her do it. Apparently they had some sort of disagreement," Bianka explained.

A moment later, a few guards moved past my room. They staring inside and that made the girls visibly uneasy.

"I'm sorry, Princess. We really have to go now," Mara said in a frightened voice. She grabbed Bianka's hand and they quickly hurried off, leaving me alone in the large, welcoming chamber. I shut the door and exhaled sharply, trying to calm my racing heart.

This was a lot to take in. Baadar must have really had a difficult life and I suspected he wanted yearned for normalcy at this point.

I thought about his tentacles and his eyes when he immersed himself in the water, naked.

Nature had blessed him with a massive cock and I swallowed hard, wondering how it would feel if he had his wicked way with me. He was so big and beautiful, his body a work of art. I wasn't even afraid of him anymore because I suddenly remembered how good he made me feel when he made me come in the water. He took my pain away and didn't even care about the fact that I was bleeding.

Still, he was a monster...

What had happened to him was cruel but it didn't change the fact that he'd thrown me in a cell after claiming he wanted to end my life. I'd never felt so confused.

My stomach growled and I suddenly realized I couldn't remember the last time I ate. I wondered if I'd be called to dinner soon.

I lay on the bed and shut my eyes, thinking that both I and Baadar had the same goal: to release ourselves fully from the curse.

He must want to become human again.

As I was drifting off to sleep, I hoped I'd see him later at dinner so I could present the proposal I had in mind. New hope filled me. I wanted to get my old life back, to return to Mount Moorhead and spend my days the way I used to. I yearned for all that was familiar, so I clung to this one speck of light that helped me believe not all was lost.

I didn't know how long I slept, but by the time I woke up, Bianka arrived to say that Baadar was waiting for me in the dining hall.

"You look beautiful in red, princess. I hope the master will like it, too," she said with a smile.

Heat jolted through me when I thought about Baadar. The monster without a stitch of clothing on, stepping into the water ... so big, so formidable. I didn't think any woman would be happy to bed him with that enormous erection, but that didn't daunt me. He made me instantly wet.

This was so inappropriate but I couldn't stop thinking about him, especially after our encounter in the pool.

Bianka was blabbing about some upcoming festival in the kingdom while I tried hard not to be nervous.

"It's here, my lady. You may go through the large wooden door. The master is waiting for you there," she said, giving me an encouraging nod.

"Thank you," I said, biting my lower lip and thinking about him bending me across the table and fucking me from behind with all his tentacles exposed.

Really, had I just lost my damn mind? Since I woke up face-to-face with Baadar, my brain had stopped functioning. All I knew was that I could feel a pull of energy between us, boosted by a dose of animalistic arousal. The fact I knew he was behind that door made it too much to bear.

I opened the door and found myself in a small, intimate dining room. Baadar was sitting behind a sizable table holding a goblet in his hand while talking to an older gentleman with a rather odd-looking beard.

"Good evening," I said.

My face flushed with heat when he stopped talking and turned to me. His piercing blue eyes seemed to look into my very soul. My cheeks burned for even the man he was talking to stared at me with open curiosity.

"Evening, Aurora. Sit, and eat," he ordered, his gaze traveling over my body while my heart threw itself over my ribcage.

I crossed over to the table and finally sat down. This dress was too revealing and my breasts threatened to spill out of it any moment. Ugh. This was going to be tricky. I should have insisted on wearing something else, but now it was too late and I really had to eat or I'd pass out.

The whole table was laden with all sorts of cooked meats, several steaming side dishes, and plenty of wine. My stomach growled once again when one of the servants approached and asked what I would like.

"Just put a bit of everything on the plate, thank you," I said.

Baadar continued to converse with the other man while I enjoyed the variety of food in front of me.

For a moment I was so caught up with eating that a moan escaped my lips. Everything was so delicious and well-seasoned.

"It's so good to see a woman that enjoys her food for once." His deep and charismatic voice brought me back to reality.

I looked around to find the other man was gone, as well as the servant, and we were alone again. Baadar was watching me from across the table, smirking, and my cheek flushed once again. He looked so handsome and debonair in the dim light. His presence did things to me I couldn't explain.

"All the dishes are scrumptious, thank you," I said, sipping some red wine. "I'm surprised you decided to put me in the chamber and not the dungeon."

"You're too fragile to be locked up, my princess. You are no use to me broken and scared," he said. "And you look stunning in that dress."

I put my fork and knife down. It was time to make my proposition. I just hoped I'd keep it together. After all, I didn't feel quite right. I was supposed to be loyal to my prince, but somehow I'd barely spared him a thought. My memories came in fits and starts, still blurry for the most part, but I remembered details here and there. I remembered I had a family—that should be enough to fight for, right? My life, whatever it had been, my loved ones, my sanity...

I laced my fingers together, thinking about the way Baadar had worshiped my body with his gaze when I stood in front of him naked. He was handsome, kind ... and so sensual. He made me want to do a lot of inappropriate things to him and I had no idea where these strange thoughts were coming from. I did not think I had ever been this wild in the past. I was, after all, a princess.

"I'm not so fragile, Baadar, and I have a proposition for you," I said in a pleasant tone.

"Proposition? I don't think you're in a position to bargain with me, princess," he muttered.

"Well, I am going to take the risk and lay all my cards on the table," I said, looking directly into his beautiful blue eyes. "It seems that we both need to track down the witch that cursed us and I guess I am safe in assuming that you would like to ask her a few questions, too."

Silence filled the room and I thought he would be

furious I'd brought this up, but his expression remained stoic. He moved his hand over his chin as his gaze lowered to my lips.

"Tell me more, princess. I could do with a beautiful distraction right now because all I can think of is you on your knees, sucking me off and swallowing my seed."

Chapter Six

B aadar

Aurora looked absolutely exquisite in that red dress that emphasized all her curves. I couldn't take my eyes off her or stop picturing her in the pool with her legs around my face. Something was brewing between us and I still didn't understand it. Her incredible scent was driving me crazy with arousal. The air changed when she entered the chamber so I quickly wrapped my conversation with Olden and sent him away.

My monster reared to be released and I didn't think I could control it. This had never happened to me before, but I knew that at some point, my monster would go into heat, unable to be controlled. The druid priests had warned me when I traveled to them because this was part of the curse, the cycle of magic. Still, I didn't feel prepared.

She nearly choked on her food when I spoke to her now. I wanted more of her and I wouldn't rest until I possessed her.

She stared at me with a mixture of horror and curiosity. I didn't want to lose control of myself. Aurora was aroused, too, and I wanted her to want me just as much. I could do so many wonderful things to her body.

Yet I couldn't forget she was still my prisoner. Nothing had changed. My plan for revenge remained in place.

We both needed to track down the last witch that wrecked both our lives. I used to thrive in the human world once. Now I was a monster most women feared, the brunt of gossip and rumors in the whole kingdom.

Aurora wasn't stupid, but she was clueless. She had no idea her beloved father, the king, was the scumbag of the century. I tracked her down and woke her up, determined to kill her—yet here she was now, sitting across from me.

"What?" she said breathlessly at last.

"You heard me," I said. "You heard me so well, I thought I'd rendered you speechless." I smirked.

"Why do you have to be so crude?" she asked, her face flushed as she continued to eat.

I laughed, wondering if the filthy prince had been the one to take her virtue. She seemed confident and I wondered if she was at all innocent where intimacy was concerned. The prince was handsome for sure, but as spoiled as he was I suspected he wasn't very experienced in the bedroom. Aurora needed to be cherished and pleased in every possible way.

"Don't tell me you have never pleasured your prince before?" I questioned, slightly amused.

Aurora sighed and stabbed the meat on her plate, her gaze averted.

"Why are you doing this to him? Why have you locked him in the dungeon like a dog? Phillip has done nothing wrong," she said, her eyes burning through my skin and igniting more fire around my groin.

All I wanted to do was bend her over this table and fill her every hole with my tentacles...

"He's my prisoner for now and he's the only person who can lead me to the last witch," I admitted, giving her some truth.

Aurora was destined to be mine years ago yet her father decided to betray me instead. I never accepted the fact that he chose to ruin my life forever, instead of fulfilling his part of the bargain.

Aurora wiped her mouth with a cloth napkin and stood. I watched as she walked round the table, getting closer to me, her scent still intoxicating and arousing. Her green eyes staring right through my soul, melting my stone cold heart. It looked like she wasn't cramping anymore and the orgasm she had gave her the necessary relief. I took my time with her as I licked her everywhere and gave her an unforgettable climax.

She was spectacular and now I was craving more.

"I know things have changed since I've been asleep, but there is a temple a little down the mountain, probably a few hours' ride from here, where powerful warlocks reside. They will direct us to the witch and who knows, they might even be able to help you remove the monster curse," she said, running her fingers over the table and biting her lips seductively.

She was going to be the death of me if she continued to tease me like that.

I grabbed her wrist as her eyes met mine and let out a low growl. "Don't play with me, princess, or you'll be sorry. If you unleash my monster, he won't show mercy. He'll take you here and now, with or without your consent."

My lips yearned to slam down on hers, but I knew

better. My monster was coming, and it was too dangerous for Aurora to be near me at this crucial moment.

A chill ran up my spine as I gazed into her dilated pupils. The heat of her stare burned right through me, making it harder for me to keep myself in check. I wanted more. Her body, her soul, everything.

"Free the prince and we will take you to the temple in the mountain," she said, and I released a small groan.

I wanted her to understand what kind of man she was promised to marry all those years ago.

"You know why your prince is locked up?" My lips curved into a wicked smile as I delivered the truth. "That slimy bastard got caught in the forest in the company of a witch who was giving him a nice, warm golden shower."

Astonishingly, she remained calm—not so much as a flinch. Did she actually understand what I just said?

"Phillip always liked unusual things," she murmured quietly and my eyes widened in surprise. Before I could utter another word, she spoke again, "You tasted my period blood earlier on."

The heat of my desire thundered through my body as she knelt before me. Though her expression remained impassive, a spark of determination blazed behind her gaze, daring me to make good on my threat and take her right then and there. I was astonished at my own control when two of my tentacles suddenly lashed out, encircling her body in their embrace. Upon contact, she gasped and locked her gaze with mine.

"You should be scared, princess," I growled out, imagining her beneath me on the table while I ravaged her. My beast would make sure she'd be sore until the morning sun rose.

"I'm not scared of you, Baadar," she said in an even tone as my tentacle ran down her spine. "But I want the prince out of the dungeon. Call your guards and let me go with them to get him out. In the morning, we both should be ready to leave for the temple."

Aurora needed to submit to me. She didn't call the shots here. Right?

Her breathing was shallow, her breasts nearly spilling out of her dress.

"Be ready at dawn because that's when we will be leaving. Guards!" I shouted and a moment later, a few of my people barged in. Aurora flinched and I got up from my chair. Her eyes shone brightly and for a second I thought she would launch herself on me and hug me tight.

Luckily, she wasn't so stupid. I didn't want her to

take pity on me. She was supposed to be my prisoner and yet, she deserved to be treated well.

"Take us to the prince," I ordered.

"Yes, my lord. Right this way," Torin, one of the guards, said, throwing a brief glance at the princess.

This was going to be interesting.

It was late evening when we entered the dungeon and darkness blanketed the forest. Aurora was full of exhilaration—and arousal, too. I could tell by her intoxicating scent that was driving me mad.

I inhaled the filthy smell of the dungeons—blood, sweat, and death. When Aurora covered her nose as she walked, I felt a good dose of shame. Dammit. But my monster fed on these scents, keeping the blood coursing through my veins.

"Phillip, it's me!" she shouted through the bars, trying to wake the stinking prince. My men left and I stayed behind, watching this scene unfold.

"Aurora, it's you! I can't believe it ... oh, and the tentacle king..." Phillip said, getting up from the corner he was hunkered in.

The cell door was open and he was free. She rushed inside and wrapped her arms around him, a gesture that had me growl in anger.

My monster was jealous because she was mine to consume and mine to play with. Phillip inhaled sharply and his hand moved fleetingly over her ass, before he looked at me and winked.

"It seems that your princess has managed to convince me to give you your freedom," I said. "We are leaving tomorrow at dawn, so don't fuck it up, otherwise you will be back in the dungeon soon enough."

Then I left because I bear to witness the way she was staring at him. Deep down I wanted her to look at me like that. I wanted to be the sole object of her desire.

Instead of walking back to my quarters, I headed to the forest to pay a visit to the alchemist.

Aurora

My voice shook as I questioned Phillip. I recalled the way he had betrayed me all those years ago, and as I looked into his eyes, my heart hardened.

He stood tall, looking pretty filthy and exhausted, his breeches hanging over his hips, revealing bruises on his abdomen. I could still see the boyish glint in his eye that I had fallen for so long ago, but the years of worldliness had chiseled away at his youthful idealism. His skin was unusually taut for someone his age, no doubt due to a concoction of magical elixirs and potions.

"Where is the witch you were caught with in the forest?" I asked, my suspicion rising.

Phillip glanced away, his cheeks tinged pink with shame. The smell of sweat and blood lingered on him, and I wanted nothing more than to go back to the castle where he could wash off the stench and rest before our journey up the mountain in search of the witch Baadar so desperately needed to find.

I couldn't fully trust Baadar yet—there was too much at stake to take any risks. The tentacle monster had allowed me to save the prince though, and I was curious as to why.

"It's been a while since I've seen that witch," Phillip muttered, raking a hand through his hair. "We met at the tavern one night. Things escalated from there."

I recalled Baadar's words—that she had put a curse on him—and wondered what role Phillip had played in our predicament.

"Perhaps it was for the best," I said, not wanting to push my luck by asking too many questions. "Baadar needs this witch to remove his monster curse, after all."

"The witch disappeared as soon as Baadar's men arrived," Phillip replied. "She used magic, and I have no idea how to find her."

I gritted my teeth as I told him that I had struck a deal with Baadar, a deal that would bind us all to his will. Phillip shook his head in disbelief, his face contorted in fear,

"Why would you do this? We're now in servitude to him and there's no guarantee we'll even find the witch!"

"Trust me Phillip, I'm doing what I have to do," I argued, my patience running thin. "The warlocks in the mountain will know where the witch is. Now let's get back to the tower so you can take a bath. You smell like a pile of horse manure!"

He stepped closer to me, his menacing gaze searching for an answer. Phillip was tall and handsome, but he didn't ignite my heart like he used to. I shuddered at the memory of Baadar's tentacles pulling me into the pool, ready to feast on my soul.

"I can think of better things for us to do than bathing, Aurora," Phillip murmured as he moved even closer.

"Of course you can," I answered, placing my hands on his chest. "But there's no time for silliness right now. Come and tell me about the kingdom and the last twenty years while we make our way back."

$$Chapter\ Seven$$

urora

Apparently my parents were still alive, but they left the mountain when Baadar began to conquer all the neighboring lands. The whole of Moorhead was invaded by his men, so my parents settled in a small coastal place away from all the drama and bloodshed.

Apparently, my father never stopped looking for me. The spell the witch cast all those years ago had me hidden away in an unknown location, Phillip claimed.

When the prince explained everything to me, my thoughts started racing. I remembered bits and pieces from my past, but overall, everything was blurry. The witch must have done something to me because my memories were in shreds. Clear one moment, elusive the next.

My father had a stepbrother who he hated with a passion—that I did recall. My father was pretty obsessed with power, but he always claimed that his stepbrother wanted to take the crown from him.

As far as I knew, I never met my uncle. Then, right after my father's coronation, there was a commotion in the main hall. Someone was trying to stop the celebration from happening. I remembered being locked in the west tower with my mother at the time.

Several hours later, the servants came to fetch us and one of the guards told my mother that everything was perfectly fine, that the person who'd caused trouble had been caught and dealt with.

Phillip claimed that he had been searching for me for years. Apparently, my father had told him that he could have my hand if he found a way to break the curse. Then he got distracted by the witch and ended up being caught by Baadar's men—which was when said witch had vanished.

We had known each other for years, since before the curse. Phillip was funny, outgoing, and a little crazy at times, but I liked spending time with him. We were never going to work as a couple, but I accepted him because it would have been a marriage of convenience, as a princess like me was duty-bound to consent to.

I had a long way ahead of me but once my curse was lifted, I could go back to my parents—with or without Phillip. Deep down I hoped to reclaim the kingdom from Baadar, but I didn't think I could challenge him just yet. I had to have a plan in place and Phillip was here to help me execute it.

He too wanted to rule over Mount Moorhead, but I couldn't imagine being his wife now after everything that happened. Men kept mistresses, but the bastard forgot about saving me because he couldn't keep his dick in his pants. He didn't have my back and I couldn't trust him, either.

Besides that, I knew I was craving the real monster, rather than the prince. I could never admit this to anyone, but it was the truth. There was an indescribable attraction between me and Baadar that I couldn't shake off.

After making sure that Phillip was in safe hands under the care of the servants, I went back to my chamber. For some reason I was exhausted, so I fell asleep pretty quickly.

Bianka and Mara woke me up at the crack of dawn and helped me get ready. We rode horses to the temple, with Baadar leading. Before we set out, my whole body reacted so strongly when I spotted the tentacle monster standing by his horse, looking more handsome than ever. He oozed strength and power.

The sun would be rising shortly on the horizon. He eyed me and Phillip for several long and unnerving moments before he barked at us to keep up our pace.

"Just admit, Aurora. I cleaned up pretty well and you can't resist me," the prince teased as we journeyed through the forest.

The soft smell of burning wood lingered in the air as we left the castle behind..

"Yes, Phillip, you have cleaned up pretty well, but you should ask the king. I'm sure he has his own opinion on the matter," I said playfully.

"I don't think so. I can see the way he's staring at you, princess. The monster wants you, there is no doubt about it."

My cheeks heated up when he said those words and erotic visions flooded my mind.

Phillip's face then clouded with uncertainty as he looked away. Baadar turned around and scanned me from head to toe, his gaze piercing and calculating.

"And how exactly is he looking at me, Phillip? Care to elaborate?" I asked when the monster finally turned his attention ahead. His eyes ... that gaze took my breath away. I swallowed hard.

"He wants you, Aurora. He wants you bad," Phillip whispered.

A long time later, we sat around a campfire. We'd ridden for hours and by the time Baadar announced that we all needed a break, I was pretty worn out. My legs and backside ached. After sleeping for so long, I wasn't used to being on a horse this much.

Once the camp was set up on the edge of the mountain, the tentacle monster vanished somewhere in the forest. I hoped we'd spend the night there. The temperature on the mountain dropped significantly and I wasn't looking forward to freezing on my horse.

"I think you're wrong. The king wants me dead, Phillip," I reminded him, feeling a sense of anticipation as I searched around for the monster.

Where had he gone off to? He'd barely spoken to me us the entire ride.

The prince took a huge bite of a chicken leg the monster had packed for us and raised an eyebrow at me.

"He wants to get his tentacles into your panties, Aurora. The monster hunger for you. Besides, why wouldn't he? You're absolutely stunning." Phillip winked at me while the juices from the meat ran down his chin.

"You got something on your face," I muttered, getting up and ignoring what he said. "I need a pee."

I walked away into the forest, needing to be alone for a moment. My heartbeat increased whenever I thought of Baadar. I should hate him, but this attraction for him was slowly driving me crazy. He was handsome and noble, despite the fact that he could turn into a tentacle monster within seconds.

His men were all humans and I knew they were watching me. Baadar had loyal servants that stayed with him for a reason. He must treat them well.

He intrigued me and I couldn't stop thinking about him. He was so powerful, yet also considerate. If I were honest, I'd admit there was nothing I wanted more than to get to know him better.

"Just don't go too far, my lady. These woods can be dangerous," one of the men said when I passed the horses, heading south.

I shivered as the temperature dropped further. I just had to hope and pray that it wouldn't start snowing because that would make this journey a lot more complicated.

I kept walking through the forest, looking for a private spot that might protect me from the elements, until I reached a clearing. Not what I had in mind. Behind it was a steep cliff, a dead end, so nowhere else to proceed. I inhaled sharply, noting the slowly settling darkness around me.

I ventured a few steps to my right with eager curiosity, but upon looking through the shrubbery, I quickly spun around in fear, my heart pounding at the sight of a man with long horns jutting out of his head and a wild gray beard. He stood between me and the unknown, challenging me to step forward into danger.

"Hello, darling, are you lost?" the man's voice sent a shudder through me. I could feel the heat radiating off his body as I took a step back, only to hit a wall of muscle behind me. The smell of whiskey, smoke, and sweat clung to his skin like a second layer, and terror gripped.

His companion went to stand next to him, just as scruffy and menacing. All my courage drained away as I realized I'd made a horrible mistake by letting my curiosity get the better of me. Now I had no escape. I swallowed hard, wishing more than anything that this was all just a nightmare I'd wake up from soon.

"No, My guards are close by," I said with fake confidence as they started to circle around me.

The first monster's raven hair contrasted with the luminous orange of his eyes. Dread tore through me as he stared at me.

"I think you're lying, little whore, and need to be

taught some manners. What do you think, Vincent?" The second monster snarled then spit on the ground, making me a little nauseous.

"Yeah, you're right. She's all alone here. How about we taste her sweet cunt and see how loud she can scream for us?" the one named Vincent stated, then he grabbed my arm and spun me around, bringing me close to his body.

Terror raced through me when he gripped my left breast tight, a second hand snaked around my waist from behind.

I screamed, reaching out with my sharp nails and raking his face. He bellowed, a sound that almost made my heart stop. My breath came in short gasps, each one filling me with more horror than the last.

But instead of freezing, I sprang into action. On impulse, I whirled around and kicked the second one as hard as I could between the legs. Both men howled in agony as I scrambled away, blood pounding in my ears.

Suddenly, Phillip burst out of the bushes, brandishing a sword. The sight brought a wave of immense relief.

Phillip bellowed in rage and raised his sword as he launched forward toward the first bastard. His blade sliced through the man's leather jerkin and blood spurted from the gash in his chest. The second one attempted an escape but he was stopped by a tremendous force that hurled him to the ground.

Phillip spun around to face a giant wolf that had just charged him then stepped back to evade the beast's attack. His sword clanged against its snarling jaws, but it was too late—the wolf had already clamped its powerful teeth down on Phillip's shoulder and proceeded to shake him like a rag doll. The last of the bandits tried desperately to escape, but he was stopped by two of the wolf's packmates and had his throat ripped out before he could take another step.

I screamed as Phillip and the wolf lunged at each other. The beast was enormous, with sharp yellow teeth and bristling fur. Spotting a knife on the ground, I scooped it up and ran toward them, spurred by fear for Phillip's safety.

I jabbed the blade into the wolf's back but as it howled in pain, I was sent flying back, crashing against a nearby tree with a force that knocked me unconscious.

When I opened my eyes, the two bandits had vanished and so had the wolves, leaving Phillip lying on the ground, drenched in his own blood. Groans of agony escaped from his throat. Baadar's men were now kneeling beside him, assessing the damage.

Wincing with pain from my own injuries, my back and ribs afire, I stood and limped over to them. If anyone was in a worse condition than me, it was Phillip.

I gasped in pain, clinging to the prince's limp body.

"We have to get him back to camp!" I shouted in desperation.

Two guards nodded and lifted the unconscious prince, then started carrying him back to our camp. Every moment we were exposed in the woods felt like a death sentence as my mind raced with visions of wild wolves descending on us.

Where is Baadar? Anger bubbled in my chest as we moved as fast as we could back to safety. When we finally arrived at the camp, the prince was gently laid down in a tent while I scurried around our provision bags, hastily gathering up healing potions for him.

"What happened?" Baadar's gruff voice bellowed from within the tent. I burst in to see him examining the prince's grave wounds. My whole body felt heavy and bruised from the ordeal, but rage still burned inside me. "We were attacked by bandits in the forest. Then wolves! Huge, wild beasts!" I seethed. "The prince saved my life while you were ... otherwise occupied."

"Those potions ... stop arguing and start using them. You're wasting time," Baadar barked.

Duly chastised, I quickly complied. Phillip's body was a mass of gruesome cuts and deep gashes, punctuated by the loss of blood that reminded me of a raging river. Before I applied the ointments, I had to clean him up. I grabbed the cloth Baadar handed me and frantically placed it on the wounds, only for it to be soaked in a matter of seconds.

Giving up, I gently poured some salve on the worst of his wounds and covered them up with fresh cloths.

At the same time, Baadar moved his hands above Phillip's body and I felt an instant warmth course through me, but the panic did not abate. Phillip was as pale as death itself, his breaths coming in shallow rasps as if his very life was slipping away.

"It's not working," I cried out. "Is he going to die?"

Baadar's eyes hardened with determination and a wolfish growl escaped his lips. His hands began to emit a brilliant light and tentacles sprouted forth from his body until they connected with Phillip. A look of intense concentration crossed Baadar's face and I watched with wonder as he weaved his magic together with Phillip's life force.

Phillip moaned in pain as the spell worked its

magic and he eventually lost consciousness again, unaware of the miracle that had just saved him.

Soon, Phillip's color returned and his breathing seemed more even.

"Now you can remove the pieces of cloth from his wounds, Aurora. I have done as much as I could—he's going to survive, but he needs rest," he said, finally raising his head and looking at me.

When I removed the soaked material, I was amazed to discover the wounds had closed up. Miracle magic had worked.

"So he is going to be all right?" I asked, barely recognizing my own voice.

"It appears so," he murmured. "My men briefly explained what happened. I had to leave the camp as a matter of safety, but now I deeply regret that," he explained—not that I understood what he meant. Did he feel he posed a threat to us?

He looked normal again, his tentacles all hidden, and his eyes shone bright blue. So beautiful my stomach fluttered and I didn't know what to do with myself.

The way he was staring at me made me a little self-conscious, for in his gaze I saw what he was thinking about—our intimate encounter at the pool.

"Yes, maybe I shouldn't have gone so far out, too,"

I confessed, taking hold of his hand. With some difficulty, I rose to my feet and gasped when a lancing pain shot through my body.

Trembling, I shut my eyes, waiting for it to pass. I heard Baadar's voice intently, his anger penetrating the air like a knife. No matter how hard I tried, I couldn't escape the agony coursing through me.

"Who did this?"

His voice reverberated in my chest and his piercing stare burned with molten rage. I could feel the intensity oozing off him like a physical force, shaking me to my core. The air felt tight and heavy with tension as I met his gaze, and I knew without a doubt that I never, ever wanted to be the target of that fury.

Chapter Eight

B aadar

I was past the point of no return as I witnessed Aurora's agony. I felt her anguish deep inside, as though we were connected. Healing the prince had drained me, but I was glad he survived. Now, the rage brought me back to myself, anchoring me again.

I'd left the camp earlier because my craving for Aurora had overwhelmed me and I became increasingly aware that if I stayed, my beast would emerge to wreak havoc—and she and my soldiers would have been in danger.

I could sense that mating season was rapidly

approaching for me, and I also noticed the way Aurora's eyes followed me around when she thought I wasn't looking, and how her heart rate accelerated whenever we accidentally touched or brushed against each other.

She was ripe and ready for the picking. I wanted to fill her cunt with my tentacles, fuck her until she couldn't walk, until she begged me to stop. But unleashing my monster could be dangerous for her, especially when I had tenuous control over my urges.

Her cheeks burned bright red and she averted her gaze when I demanded to know who hurt her. Once everything was sorted here at camp, I would track the bastards who attacked Aurora and make them pay for daring to lay a finger on what belonged to me.

"The wolf must have shoved me when I was trying to stop him from hurting Phillip," she answered, finally looking up at me.

This was shaping up to be the longest night of my life.

"Come here, princess. Let me see what we are dealing with," I ordered.

She gasped when I pulled her to the back of the tent, away from the prince. He was stable for now, which was good because my attention was fixed on Aurora.

"I'm just exhausted. You don't have to worry about me," she assured, biting on her bottom lip.

This woman, along with her supposed prince, was going to be the death of me. I found myself burning up at the sight of her worrying her lip.

"Be silent and take off your dress," I demanded, snatching her wrist and pulling her against my body. I immediately knew this was a bad idea. My body temperature skyrocketed and I wanted to rip off her clothes and take her here and now.

Also, she winced in pain.

Dammit!

She inhaled a deep breath. "My ribs are injured but I should be okay in a few days," she replied, blushing fiercely. She was trying to mask her arousal, but I could sense the fire between us. She needed my tentacles, begging for them to fill her in every hole.

First though, to make her all better.

"You need to let me heal you now, so be a good girl and take off your dress," I ordered, lowering my voice.

The prince was asleep and we had all night. No one was going to dare to attack the camp, not after what I had done to one of the wolfmen.

When her dress dropped to the ground and I saw all the bruises, the ugly evidence of the violence on her body, I could barely control the rage surging through me. Her left side, once glowing with health, was now a mass of black-and-blue contusions. Dried blood stained her skin in small rivulets, a testament to her suffering. My eyes roved hungrily over her pert breasts, their nipples poking through the fabric of her undergarments like arrows, and I had to grit my teeth to keep my inner beast at bay. This wasn't the time...

"That looks worse than it feels," Aurora said.

"Don't lie to me, Aurora. I know you're in pain. Now let me release my tentacles and heal you, princess," I growled. I didn't even fucking know why I cared, but I was past questioning that. We only had one tent set up for me, but after what happened, Aurora wasn't going to be sleeping outside in the cold.

She looked hesitant, but she wasn't scared of me. Besides, she already knew what to expect after seeing me in my monster form in the bath. She tasted unbelievable and her sweet scent was still driving me crazy.

"What are you going to do to me?" she whispered, her dark eyes searching mine. It felt as though she could see right through me, and being so vulnerable immobilized me with fear.

"Heal you, my dearest princess," I murmured, my voice heavy with emotion.

Then, without warning, tentacles sprouted from my body, spreading in all directions like webs of black silk. Her gasp echoed in my ears and I wanted to do more than just heal her.

The tentacles wrapped around her legs, thighs and waist, lifting and turning her so she was lying flat. Her eyes were wide with a mixture of excitement and a hint of terror. I could feel the thunderous beat of her heart against her chest and the heat radiating from her core as her desire for me grew stronger, even through the fear.

"You are beautiful," I said softly, wanting so badly for her to touch me with her lips or feel the caress of my mating tentacle.

Her body trembled as I spoke the words and I could tell she felt the same primal yearning.

A thought hit me then ... if only Phillip were awake to watch me with Aurora. Maybe he'd learn a thing or two about what made her tick.

That idea struck me as wonderfully erotic. I was so high strung, I might let him join, as long as he did what I asked like a good little boy...

She took a deep breath and opened her eyes, showing me she did trust me, despite her apprehension. My monster stirred within me, ready and hungry.

I began to heal her wounds, carefully pushing warm energy over her bruised skin until the marks began to fade away. Her body shivered beneath my touch, and the scent of roses and tulips lingered in the air like summer rain.

She moaned silently when I guided the warmth down between her legs.

My beast grew as I worked, threatening to be released, and I started panting. I didn't think I could control myself being so close to her. Aurora's body was responding so well to my touch that it was difficult for me to stay still.

She was so aroused by my tentacles and the blood was rushing to my cock. My body burned, especially when the tentacles slid around her body. I felt every movement, every whimper, and every breath she took. I felt the thrill of unleashing my inner beast, the sensation of her skin against mine, the tantalizing pleasure that came with each touch.

But I knew my actions were wrong, and with each moan I heard her heart breaking as I was betraying her trust, using my healing ministrations as a way to slake my desires.

A deep sense of guilt slowly ate away at my joy as I reveled in the forbidden pleasure.

"You're so exquisite, my dear Aurora, and my beast needs you," I blurted out, unable to think. I had to consume her, with my body and my soul. She was mine to take care of, mine to touch, and mine to please.

Phillip was lying there, barely hanging on, and I wanted to make her body feel alive with pleasure. She was still menstruating, but I found that strangely alluring. Her blood tasted like ambrosia. Another tentacle emerged from my body, slowly stroking her thigh, and she smelled like a summer storm in full bloom.

My cock ached as the tentacle teased her through her undergarment. She opened her eyes, blushing as she stared at me.

"Baadar, I'm so hot, I'm burning... Please touch me," she begged.

I wanted this as much as she did, but it was wrong. I couldn't do this, then get rid of her. End her life. Everything was happening so fast and confusion had taken the reins.

Deep down I kept telling myself that I hated her because of who she was, but life was never that simple. The human side of me had already claimed this woman as mine—despite who and what her father was.

I used my other tentacles to spread her legs wider. Her panties were soaked through, even with the pad, and that just made me go even wilder because I wanted to fill her every hole and fuck her until she couldn't take it anymore, until she was begging me to stop.

I leaned into her ear and growled, "You're ready for me, princess, and you love it when my tentacle ravages your tight little hole, you dirty slut." Not giving her time to respond, I slid my tentacle inside her clothing and then deep inside her, slinking within her walls that pulsated with need.

Every moan, every quiver of her body filled me with aching pleasure. Pre-cum seeped from my tentacle as I thrust deeper and harder into her.

Finally, I ripped off her underwear with a second tentacle and she gasped in delight. Her chest heaved with each stroke and her eyes rolled back in rapture. She looked so beautiful beneath me, completely at my mercy. I purred in pleasure as her tight walls squeezed my tentacle, wishing she could feel the same pleasure that coursed through me.

"Do you want me to make you come? Will you beg for me to fuck you? Or do you want your injured prince to take you instead?" I pressed my smaller tentacle against her opening and thrust. Her body accommodated my size as a third tentacle danced over her clit. An inferno of desire burned in my veins.

"No, I want you and only you right now. Oh, for Gods this feels so good," she said, arching her head backwards.

I continued to thrust inside her, noting her nipples had gone stiff as she neared orgasm. She was moaning so loud, my men were probably hearing her outside. A trickle of sweat dropped down my face as I bared my teeth. She was being held in place by my tentacles, the smaller one fucking her cunt hard and fast.

Then we were both exploding as I picked up the pace. Pleasure spread through my body and I ejaculated inside her, emitting a loud roar. Aurora screamed then came hard, once, twice, and then multiple times until I pulled the tentacle, trying to catch my breath.

She trembled in my arms, both our breathing heavy and erratic. I had pleasured many mortal women before, but few could withstand my beast. This time, however, things happened instinctually. My beast was hungry, yet all the while it felt like she was made for me.

I loathed the pain my curse caused the women in my past, yet I'd been completely powerless to stop it. Aurora was ... different.

Was this fate?

"Are you all right, my princess?" I asked, wanting nothing more than to kiss her now. The tent reeked of our lovemaking, and though my men would smell it for days, this was a small price to pay for the sheer pleasure she had given me.

She slowly opened her eyes, her chest heaving, clearly exhausted from our passion.

"I've never felt better," she breathed out as I laid her

down beside the prince. We only had the one tent, so I decided to sleep with both of them since Phillip still needed time to heal.

"You're sending me into heat," I warned her, trying to be gentle despite the severity of the situation.

"What does that mean?" she asked, seemingly dazed by all she had seen.

I let out a heavy sigh, no longer seeing a reason to try and protect her from the truth.

I'd never felt such intense urges before so I knew ... this was it.

The curse's mission was coming to a head.

"It means that I need to find my mate soon or else I will die," I declared solemnly.

Chapter Nine

A urora

We didn't speak after that. I was too spent to take time to analyze what he'd just said. My body was sated, happy, and I'd never felt this way before.

Baadar slept next to me and Phillip was on my other side, still breathing evenly. At first I was a little embarrassed by the fact that I let him fill me with his terrifying tentacles—what kind of a pervert was I? But those were a part of him and I'd never orgasmed harder. And so many times, too.

Sleep came quickly as I nestled against his enormous and warm body, feeling safe and calm. This had been the most bizarre and profound experience of my life.

I was a princess, trained and expected to guard my virtue, yet I was inexorably drawn to explore my burgeoning sexuality. Before my whole world collapsed, I'd been a rebel who secretly questioned the rules and never saw a reason to hold myself back. My encounters with other men had been quite pleasurable, but none of them ever managed to awaken me the way tentacle monster had.

As I succumbed to a deep, dreamless sleep, fantasies of him and I together as he slowly lifted his curse danced through my mind.

The morning sun rose too quickly and when I awoke, Baadar was nowhere to be seen. Memories of the night before flooded back, and I felt a tingle in all of my sensitive spots. A dull ache lingered in my body, telling me that he had indeed possessed me and worked his intimate magic on me.

His tentacles were slimy and sticky yet strangely comforting as he played my body like an instrument, with tenderness and strength in equal measure. The pleasure he brought was overwhelming, pushing me to the brink of sanity until I reached an orgasmic bliss beyond anything I could ever have imagined.

"You're awake?" Phillip's deep voice had me stiffening. I slowly turned to face him. His strong arms were wrapped around me, but my heart wasn't beating for him. I knew he was expecting me to make good on our marriage arrangement so he could become king, but his touch would never compare to the passion Baadar stirred within me. I had slept with Phillip before, but it was never as satisfying as when Baadar had me pinned down with his tentacles.

"I'm here," I said softly, sitting up on the bed.

My dress from yesterday was still neat and crease free. I must have put it on sometime last night, as well as a new pair of underwear and protection for my bleeding. Had I changed, or did Baadar put the clothing on me?

"I'm feeling better now—a bit achy and bruised. What happened last night? I don't remember much," he asked.

I told myself that he probably didn't remember a thing and even if he heard something, he wouldn't be able to put two and two together.

"You came to my rescue when the bandits surrounded me," I explained, wondering where Baadar was now. I really had to thank him for what he had done for me earlier and for saving Phillip's life, too. "Then you were attacked by the wolf and I thought he would kill you... I tried to get him off you, but I couldn't..."

"Ah, Aurora, why would you do such a thing? The wolf could have killed you," Phillip said, stretching his arms and yawning loudly, then his face twisted with pain. He was probably going to ache for a little while—after all he'd been nearly torn to pieces by a dangerous beast. I was amazed that all his deep cuts were healed and only dried blood remained.

We both needed a bath and I was hoping the temple wasn't too far ahead since we'd already traveled quite a distance. I quickly explained to Phillip what happened after Baadar and his men arrived. I told him how he'd healed him, leaving out all the other, saucy details about us.

I bit my lip, thinking about the monster. He was the rightful king of Moorhead because he took the crown from my father, and now he needed a mate to survive. What did this mean for me?

This whole thing sounded very complicated and we still weren't any close to tracking down the last witch in Moorhead. I let out a long sigh, feeling overwhelmed by the sudden turn of events. There was so much to take in, and it felt like we were so far from reaching any solution.

"I guess I have to thank him," Phillip admitted dismally.

"Yes, he saved both our lives and also woke me up from my sleep," I said, not wanting to talk about the deal I'd made with him. He was a monster yet I did care about him. I just wasn't sure exactly how much.

Phillip left the tent as though he'd only suffered scrapes in the fight with the wolf. Luckily, we were traveling with a few of Baadar's servants. Bianka brought me some new attire to put on. She didn't ask questions, but I kept blushing when I thought about last night.

"You will ride with me. The horses got away last night. My men found most of them but were unable to retrieve yours, Aurora," Baadar said when I finally came out of the tent.

My stomach was growling, so Bianka handed me some cold meat, along with a glass of water. His men must have been preparing since the early morning to get back on the road.

My heart skipped a beat and then raced triple time when Baadar stood in front of me, looking so handsome. Always the same reaction. Who would have thought what my fate would be like once I awoke? The witch who put a curse on me had made the castle disappear for years, so no one could ever find me.

But *he* did.

"Are we leaving right away?" I asked. The sun was shining and it was warm—a silver lining. Normally, this part of the kingdom experienced some harsh climate, but it was the end of the fall. Soon, winter would be here and the weather would worsen a great deal.

Baadar's stare was like a blade, cutting my soul in two as he spoke. I saw the warmth in his eyes, melting away the numbing frost I'd caught in his gaze before. He explained we had a few hours' journey ahead of us until we reached our destination. A chill ran through my body as I comprehended the importance of what he meant. We'd be at the temple soon.

My stomach tied in knots. Once Baadar was freed from his curse, would he still want me? He only wanted a mate so he wouldn't die, but if he returned to being human, he'd have no use for me. We were destined to be separated, while I had to fulfill my duty and fight for the throne with Phillip by my side. But this realization didn't help me feel at all better. More despondent, if anything.

"I can ride with Phillip," I said, struggling to keep my emotions in check.

"No, you're riding with me," he said with a smile

that made my heart flutter. "Phillip is still healing and I want to keep an eye on you."

I wanted to ask him questions about why it was so crucial that he found a mate, but he was already turning away from me.

"Are you going to tell me more about this whole mating thing?" I asked him later on as we continued to ride, our bodies flush together.

His men were around us and Phillip was up ahead, talking to Bianka and looking quite fine.

Why did Baadar want me to ride with him? My palms were slick with sweat and my heart hammered in my chest as I thought back to the night before ... when he'd given me so much pleasure. I suddenly wondered how his cock would feel inside me.

"Mating," he started, leaning closer so his breath warmed my cheek, "means that my monster must mate with a female soon or he won't survive, for I have cursed blood."

The conflict between my fear and desire for Baadar was addling my brain. I wasn't sure which feeling was stronger.

"Can you elaborate?" I asked. Why did he have to smell so good?

He growled deep in his throat as he spoke, his every word sending shockwaves of desire through my body.

"Fucking. Hard fucking that will last for days and by the end of it, you will be with child. But my beast is too much for a mere human female to handle."

His eyes burned with intensity. I imagined us in bed, our bodies locked together in the throes of passion. The thought of him ravaging me until I was completely wrecked by his power made my core tremble with anticipation.

"Days?" I breathed, barely able to utter the word. I thought I'd be able to survive anything after last night —maybe I was stronger than he believed. "You're thinking about it, princess, aren't you? I can smell your arousal. Would you be willing to sacrifice yourself like that for me?"

He was much closer now if it was even possible. Heat radiated from his body. Our eyes met and I felt a spark, an electrifying energy that sent shivers down my spine. This was wrong on so many levels, yet I couldn't help but want him. The tension between us was palpable and it felt like I was going to burst. This was how it would always be between us...

...until he changed...

His eyes glowed.

"I think you know after last night that I can handle your dark power," I bravely declared.

Shifting on the saddle, he snaked his hand to my

chest and pinched my nipple. I gasped at the unexpectedness of it.

"Stop tempting me, Aurora," he warned. "You have no idea what you are asking for. I have killed many women while copulating with them and you should know that your fate would be the same! Do not test me. As much as I hate to say this, surrender your dreams of being with me and go back to Phillip, your future king."

He went silent then, leaving me to ponder his words. Whatever came out of his mouth meant one thing, yet his eyes and body said another. Why was he doing this?

My voice was a sharp blade slicing through the air as I countered, "I don't want Phillip and I can handle anything." Contempt laced my tone.

His booming laugh did something to me. I wanted to hear his laughter so bad, it made me ache. Phillip and Bianka both froze, turning to take in the scene. Baadar succumbing to a bout of humor—not something anyone saw very often, it seemed.

My mind backtracked on what he'd just told me. He couldn't be serious ... or could he? It seemed to me that if he'd killed before, I should think twice about what I wanted. Beneath my facade of bravery, I knew that if he chose to use those tentacles and unleash the monster inside, he could easily break me.

"You amaze me, princess, but this will never come to be. Thank heavens the curse will soon be broken before the mating ritual is required," he said firmly.

There were so many questions I wanted to ask him, but we had to move on as a few of his men rushed back to us, shouting about an injured comrade. Baadar hastily pushed me off his horse and galloped away toward the trees ahead.

"Quickly, Aurora, you can ride with me this time. I swear I will keep you safe," Phillip urged while helping me mount his wide steed.

My body was still overcome with sensations of warmth and desire, yet I welcomed the sudden relief from Baadar's icy demeanor. Now at least we knew each other better.

"What do you suppose happened back there?" I whispered.

"It definitely seems like the work of warlocks," Phillip said solemnly. "They like to leave traps all over these parts and one of his minions must have fallen into one." His golden gaze was heavy on me, filled with concern. "You look a bit frazzled, Aurora. Are you sure you're all right?"

I tried to stay calm and collected, but my mask was

slipping. Still, I forced a smile and shook my head. "I'm fine, Phillip. You know I can take care of myself, right? Now let's just focus on finding that witch."

The prince nodded resolutely and we continued our ride for two more hours until the clearing in the valley came into view. On top of the hill we spotted an old warlock temple and Phillip started tickling me in an attempt to distract me from my thoughts about Baadar. He seemed to be more perceptive than he let out.

"I need to taste one theory, Aurora, so just play along with it," he said when we were getting closer to the huge gate. Baadar was there, talking to what appeared to be a bunch of warlocks.

"What are you—"

He didn't wait for me to turn around before he reached out and grabbed my face, then kissed me on the lips with a passion that left me stunned. His tongue danced with mine while I attempted to process what was happening, but my mind was too overwhelmed by his touch, his scent, and the heat radiating from his body.

His grip was tight and unyielding, refusing to let me go until we reached the gate. When he finally released me, the air rushed out of my lungs and my skin burned with unexpected desire. The kiss was rough and needy, but when I came to my senses, I realized I was more shocked than aroused by Phillip's actions.

His gaze met mine, amusement flashing in his eyes, while Baadar looked on, unimpressed and furious at the same time. I didn't think this was going to end well for both of us.

My heart raced as I tried to compose myself, but the blush that crept to my cheeks must have given away my confusion. Phillip only chuckled quietly, his expression dripping in mischief that only the two of us could understand.

"Warlocks are waiting for you, Prince Phillip," Baadar barked as we approached him.

One of the warlocks, an elderly man with a long silver beard, gave me a polite smile. Despite my puzzlement and temporary brain fog, I couldn't deny the thrill that filled my chest.

I had no idea what kind of game Phillip was playing, but it was obviously dangerous, judging from the bloodthirsty look in Baadar's eyes.

Still, I couldn't help but feel drawn in by the excitement of it all. There was no doubt I'd completely lost my mind.

Chapter Ten

B^{aadar}

Rage surged through me like a raging inferno when my eyes locked with Phillip's while he kissed Aurora. Every part of me wanted to rip him apart. The audacity of him to claim something that was rightfully mine, to put his vile mouth on her sweet lips and run his filthy hands over her body.

My knuckles whitened as I fisted my hands and my heart pounded with maniacal fury as I contemplated the thought of pulling Aurora out of his arms and claiming her right there, in front of the whole world.

He finally pulled away from her, and Aurora's

cheeks were flushed as she tried to gather herself. He truly had a death wish. I sensed his desire for her, but he couldn't fool me. He'd only done this to get a rise out of me.

The prince's smirk sent a shudder of revulsion through me and I dreamed of destroying his face until it was nothing more than a bloody pulp, then reduce his remains to ash. I had no time to avenge Aurora last night, but tonight I was planning to track down the bandits who'd attacked her in the forest. No one could escape the wrath of the tentacle monster.

"Hello Jospeh, lead away. I believe we haven't seen each other for ages, so it would be good to catch up," Phillip said to one of the warlocks that didn't seem too pleased with the fact that we arrived unannounced.

I didn't give a damn about warlocks. They were guests on my family's land and they still answered to us. If they refused to help, I could reduce their fancy temple to rubble with a single wave of my hand. I wouldn't rest until this place, with all its stone columns and imposing sculptures were nothing but dust in the wind.

The prince stepped toward me, eyes afire and a predatory smirk on his lips. Bending closer, he whispered in my ear, "Don't worry, Baadar. I'll warm her up for you and she'll taste as sweet as I remember."

Then he walked off before I could push him against the wall and make him choke on my tentacle. I could destroy him as much as I could bring him back to life, but he was wrong about him calling any shots where Aurora was concerned. His fate now lay in my hands, and I was ready to end him.

I started barking orders at my men, who quickly realized I was in a bad mood because they all scurried away, pretending to get busy with their usual duties.

I was allowing the prince to test me and my patience, and this wouldn't do. Moments later, it was just me and the princess left in the temple courtyard. Phillip had walked away with the warlocks.

Aurora looked surprised and embarrassed about Phillip's lack of manners. At this point I needed to put distance between us in order for my inner beast not to take over. I'd often been told about going into heat and what it could do to me. The last semblance of humanity that I had was on the verge of being completely obliterated—forever.

In the midst of all this, there was Aurora, the woman I couldn't stop craving.

"Baadar ... I am sorry. He caught me off guard. I wasn't expecting him to kiss me," Aurora said as we walked inside the temple.

The walls around us felt electric with the power

that pulsated through the air. I let out two slim tentacles that writhed in anticipation, a sign of the transformation I was beginning to undergo. Grabbing her waist, I pushed her against the wall and ran one tentacle down her cheek. She was fucking beautiful and tempting, her pussy throbbing with the need for release.

She was eager to taste me again, as she had in the tent when she exploded all over my tentacles, then begged for more. I inhaled her sweet arousal as she clenched her thighs together, desperately wanting me to take her as my mate. I understood her plea—she was offering herself up to me.

The rage within me burned brighter than anything else and I knew what I had to do.

Rage and hunger like no other. I was tired of holding back. Tired of denying myself...

A dark smile spread across my lips as I forced her legs apart and pressed my hard erection against her. She gave a sharp gasp and I could sense the terror radiating off her as I leaned close and growled, "You better not be lying to me, princess. Now open your mouth for me like the good girl you are."

She shook her head, staring at me like I'd lost my fucking mind—and maybe I truly had at this point. I had never felt this kind of attraction toward anyone else. Only her. The need to consume her, body and soul, was unbearable.

Her eyes widened in horror as I unleashed the monster that lived within me, a creature of pure primal desire. Her warmth and tenderness drove me ever closer to the edge. I needed her like I needed sustenance, with an insatiable hunger that terrified even me.

"You liked it when I fucked you with my tentacle back in the tent. Well now let me fuck your mouth." I slid my tentacle between her lips. "That's it. I knew you could take it. This is an extension of my cock, so show me what you'd do if I let you suck it, princess," I said, pushing my tentacle all the way into the back of her throat.

She shook her head and tears started streaming down her face as I held her so tight, she couldn't budge. I trailed my hands over her chest, squeezing both breasts while I continued to abuse her stunning mouth.

She gagged, a sound so sensual, I damn near lost control. She felt like heaven in my arms, choking on my appendage and pleading with her eyes to stop.

She didn't understand that she already belonged to me and the need to mate with her was filling me with guilt. The threat this posed to her still eluded her. I had to show her what she was getting into because I couldn't stay away.

"You're doing so well..." I rasped. "Do you want me to come into your mouth so you can feel the intensity of my passion for you? This is what it'll be like if I make you mine. No hearts and flowers—just pure, hard fucking."

I withdrew the tentacle from her mouth to get a grip on myself. Her expression registered dread, her eyes watered, and her lush lips were swollen.

"You wouldn't hurt me," she whispered at last.

Yet her tone was tinged with uncertainty. She glimpsed the darkness in me—the monster inside. I should not want her because she was destined to die at my hand. Maybe I could scare her away.

"You're so pathetic. Look at you, soaking wet for me because you want to prove to yourself that you can handle me. But the truth is that no mortal woman will ever be able to," I snarled.

After watching Phillip touch her, I saw red. Clearly, I didn't pass the composure test. And for what? This could never be. If Aurora knew the full truth about me, how much of a danger I posed to her, she'd have continued to hate me.

I tore away from her, my feet pounding the floor as I put as much distance between us as I could.

Yet, when she was beyond eyesight and I was no longer in her presence, her emotions permeated my soul—a wild concoction of fear, need, and longing. I wanted her to despise me, to feel nothing but loathing for me. Instead, she was desperate for my acceptance and desire. I wanted to save us both from the pain of what could be, yet the hurtful words dangling from my mouth tasted like ashes in the air.

I kept on walking, trying not to think about the way she felt in my arms and how hard she tried not to enjoy my tentacle, yet was constantly betrayed by her carnal instincts. Aurora was like an open book, at least for me. Even if I tried not to read her, I understood her to the depths of my soul.

I continued to breathe through my anger, clenching my fists, forcing myself to tame my beast, the monster that was part of me.

The prince was talking to the warlocks in the main hall, so I decided to head over to them. Aurora would probably be shown to her chamber soon. One of the servants must have found her by now.

I wondered if the anger was mostly directed at myself. I should be repentant for my feelings, but I couldn't allow myself to feel that way. I ached for her to be my mate, but I feared for the transformation my inner beast may wreak if I succumbed to such feelings.

The agony of not being able to love her, yet wanting her so badly, threatened to rip me apart.

She would gladly suck my cock, but would she marry me? I didn't think so because at the end of the day, I was who I was. If we married, her father would have had a fit. Maybe he'd see it as a worse punishment than if I executed her. I wanted to see his face when he found out that I was still alive and that I took everything from him. His kingdom, his daughter.

I tread through empty corridors. This place was enormous, filled with ancient magic that drifted on the surface of my skin. Even my monster sensed it.

I knew the witch had visited this temple before, so it was just going to be a matter of time before we tracked her down.

I just had to hope that Aurora wouldn't get lost in this big old place. I told myself that I wasn't supposed to care. She was a grown woman and meant nothing to me. Whatever I felt was a purely physical response.

She was probably sobbing in her chamber, trying to convince herself that I needed her and she couldn't leave me just yet. I didn't feel her emotions right then though, so that left me in an even worse mood.

At last, I found the main hall where Phillip was conversing with warlocks.

The spacious chamber was lined on one side with a

wide, floor-to-ceiling glass wall, bringing the outdoors in. The view was magnificent. The mountain dominated the landscape, a scant number of trees clinging to its slopes in this area. Three warlocks, the prince, and a few of my men were gathered in the room.

The prince winked at me when I entered. What an odd man he was. Everyone was frightened of me, but he wasn't in the least. His eyes glimmered as they settled on my form and I finally confirmed: He didn't want Aurora, not really. He only toyed with her because she benefited him. In truth, he was after the crown.

"The king is here!" Phillip bellowed, and my men, along with the warlocks, dropped to their knees, paying me the homage I so rightly deserved. I could see in their eyes a deep-seated terror for my fury was palpable and too powerful to ignore. The warlocks, who thought themselves masters of magic, had finally learned the lesson to dread the great power I wielded.

My rage boiled up like magma inside me, and I snarled.

"Don't waste my time! I need to find that witch. Just direct me to the witch so we can part ways!"

One warlock with a long white beard that I hadn't seen before adjusted his cape nervously before answering.

"The witch is hidden within the mortal world, but if we offer her the right reward—the power of immortality—she will accept it. We are here to discover what motivates her. What would she desire more than anything else?"

I waited for an answer, my patience wearing thin.

Suddenly, Joseph, the younger warlock, spoke up. "It's the firelight! The ancient light from the depths of Hell that will make her immortal. That's why she's here—she's been searching for it all this time!"

"So, how do we acquire this firelight?" I demanded, watching as Phillip's lips curved in a smile. He didn't realize he was playing with fire, acting this way, so flippantly especially when he teased Aurora in front of me.

The warlocks exchanged glances, their faces filled with concern. "We do not know the answer to that yet."

"Well, find it," I growled.

Finding themselves with nothing more to say, they bid us farewell, inviting us to join them for dinner later.

I quickly instructed my men to go prepare for our morning departure. Now I had a clear goal. I knew how to entice the last witch. I could find out how to go about that myself, so we didn't need to stay here for long and waste any more time than necessary.

As the prince and I were left in the chamber alone, I was hit with a twisted and mad idea. Or rather, my monster was. It was a cruel thought, but I wanted to know how far he'd go with his display of fake loyalty to reach his own ends. Or was I wrong and he really did want the princess for himself?

I knew the outcome of this night would be the deciding factor, and it scared me more than anything I had ever faced before. All I could do was hope he would take the bait and I'd follow through with my plan. I'd hazard to guess he'd be game since it catered to his hedonistic nature. But I could be wrong, couldn't I?

What I couldn't deny was the lengths of insanity and depravity I'd go to in order to own the woman that wouldn't leave my daylight and nighttime dreams.

Chapter Eleven

urora

I was pretty shaken when one of the servants that worked for the warlocks showed me the way to my chamber. Baadar's assault left me deeply worried and ... very aroused. His angry face flashed through my mind as I tried to settle in.

What had I become? And most importantly, what fate awaited me? His jealous wrath had been palpable and I could feel it beating against me like a hot, blustery wind. I shuddered at the thought of crossing him again, even though Phillip had caught me off guard with that kiss. I was not expecting such a bold move from him, although I remembered how he liked teasing other men that were particularly interested in me. This time, however, his actions were foolish and put both of us in jeopardy. With Baadar so furious, it might have ended badly for Phillip and me.

My large chamber had everything I needed in it, mainly the comfortable bed. I wasn't sure what I was supposed to do with myself until dinner time. Should I explore or stay put? Maybe I should remain cooped up here so I wouldn't run the risk of running into Baadar. I wasn't ready to face him just yet.

Baadar was possessive and brutal, but deep down, despite his monstrous nature, he had a kind heart. Maybe I was crazy in thinking he wouldn't hurt me when he was in his monster form, but I had always been good at reading people.

Granted—people, not monsters.

I lay on the bed, thinking about what he had done and said earlier on. What always surprised me the most was my body's primal reaction to his touch. I got so wet when he forced me to suck on his massive tentacle. Uncomfortable and wet.

He admitted that it was an extension of his cock and after seeing him naked, I could vouch that the shaft in question was enormous. My mouth watered when I thought about just how well he could satisfy me. I enjoyed sucking him off more than I realized, but it wasn't enough.

I wanted to please him more than any other woman in the world. In fact, I wanted him to forget about any other woman.

Thoughts of the future filled me with uncertainty. We both wanted to be free of the curse. I hoped that once it was all over, Baadar would let me go.

My eyelids drooped heavily and I felt myself slipping into dreamland. The dreams soon came to visit. Terrifying at first, when long, slimy tentacles each felt like a viper's embrace, caressing me with their poisonous touch. But then, everything changed, becoming more alluring. Exciting. His lovemaking was rough and wild and seemed to go on for eternity—yet I never feared his monstrous form... I had an unbreakable trust in him. When I finally woke up, I somehow felt better and more rested.

We were high in the mountains, so it was cold and nippy, especially at nighttime. When I glanced out the window, it was pitch dark. I shivered, then quickly wrapped a blanket around my body.

I needed to speak to Phillip about his conversation with the warlocks. I liked being kept in the loop. Baadar might still be in a nasty mood, so I wanted to avoid him if necessary.

I wandered outside my chamber, barefoot, hoping to find a servant. I was a little hungry, too. The corridors were empty, cold and dark. I swallowed hard as I continued searching for another soul, wondering what time it was. Everyone was probably fast asleep already. This whole place was filled with potent magic. I could sense it drifting around me, moving over my body, making the hair rise at the back of my neck.

I went to the ground floor, looking for the kitchen where I hoped to fill my belly. I quickly realized I must have taken the wrong turn because I ended up in some sort of washroom, similar to Baadar's.

In front of me was a large pool filled with roses and lilies. I walked around it, my face flushing as the memory of Baadar holding me with his tentacles while he feasted on my pussy came to the forefront of my mind. For a while he pretended he didn't care about my feelings, but I saw through him right away.

So many conflicted emotions assailed me. I had to be careful, watch out for myself, because there was something about Baadar that left me uneasy and I couldn't pinpoint what it was. I wanted him, couldn't deny that, but committing to be his mate—that was another story. Everything was going too fast.

Besides, I was here alone with so many men—

Baadar's people, the warlocks. This was unfamiliar territory.

I stared at the pool, tempted to strip and dive in, but an inner voice sent alarm bells ringing in my head. When I heard the door creak open, I froze for a second, then frantically searched for a place to hide. To make matters worse, it was Baadar entering with Phillip. Desperate, I found refuge within the shadows of an alcove, behind an enormous vase.

"So what's your plan, Phillip?" Baadar asked, and my heart pounded in my chest. Phillip was a master of manipulation and I had a feeling that this conversation was going to take a twisted turn.

He grinned wickedly at Baadar, who seemed tense and rigid as he stared into the pool. In a flash, he whipped his shirt off and I gasped at his broad, muscled chest. My throat went dry and desire struck instantly.

Oh dear.

What were they doing here in the dead of night?

"We need to get her the firelight if we want her to come," Phillip uttered, a possessive gleam in his eyes as he scanned Baadar's body.

I was seriously considering fleeing my hidey-hole, but how? Things would get even worse if they caught me spying on them but if I moved, there was no way they wouldn't notice. I couldn't see any other exit out of here, either.

Baadar slowly peeled off the rest of his clothes, revealing every inch of his body to the prince. Phillip stared wide-eyed and transfixed, as Baadar's rippling muscles glinted in the light. The air between them crackled with charged anticipation.

Wait, what?

Baadar entered the pool, quickly immersing himself in the water with gentle strokes that belied the monster lurking within. With every movement, a sinister energy exuded from him, its strength threatening to suck out all the air in the room. Phillip seemed to have succumbed to a mesmerized lust. I was shocked to see he was actually turned on by the tentacle monster.

Shocked and horrified, yet wild horses couldn't drag me away at this point.

Baadar's icy gaze shifted to the alcove and it was like he knew I was here. I held my breath, praying I was wrong and he really didn't see me. But then, an evil smirk—couldn't describe it as anything different—crossed his face, and I knew then he was playing with me. He probably knew I'd been here the entire time.

Phillip and Baadar exchanged a glance, and something about it rubbed me the wrong way.

"Master Atkin knows. He's the eldest of the warlocks," Phillip said, watching the king like a hawk.

Could the two of them have bonded when Baadar had healed him? If he didn't care, he would have just let him die that day, but he didn't.

"Are you going to get in, Phillip? You need to wash the dirt from today's long journey. We are leaving tomorrow morning and I don't think there will be another chance to take a bath soon enough," Baadar stated, drifting around the water.

I raised my hands to my chest as if that would calm the frantic beating of my heart.

Phillip stripped his clothing, moving leisurely as if peeling away his inhibitions, until he stood in all his naked glory. His body had aged, yet still contained a well-honed attractiveness that would make any woman's heart flutter.

I held my breath as both men stared at each other for a long moment. I didn't even dare to swallow for the air crackled with tension. For too long, none of them moved or made a sound.

Phillip was going to be my husband. He was the man my father had chosen for me, but now I didn't think I could ever be with him, especially after being so intimate with Baadar. And even more so after seeing the way he looked at the monster. Clearly, he was into men. Or perhaps into *this* particular man.

The tentacle monster swam to the edge of the pool then stepped out, shaking the water out of his hair. His skin was a thing of beauty when wet. He narrowed the distance between him and Phillip, standing quite a few inches taller and frankly, dwarfing the man.

My heart raced in my chest as I waited with a mixture of dread and excitement, wondering how this would play out. Phillip's bold kiss had enraged Baadar, and now the monstrous tentacle creature was consumed with jealousy and a possessive urge.

"Do you desire Aurora for yourself, Prince?" Baadar asked, touching Phillip's cheek.

Both men were naked and gorgeous, but I doubted Phillip had anticipated this when the king summoned him. His chest rose and fell in rapid movements.

My gaze shifted to Phillip's stiff member, then I noticed Baadar's tense muscles as he stood with his back to me. Suddenly, my own body decided the scene before me was desire incarnate and reacted accordingly.

I curled my toes and pressed my thighs together when a trickle of juice made its way down my leg. I slipped my hand down between my legs and inhaled sharply.

"She has always been beautiful, but I believe

Aurora isn't ready to fulfill all my needs. She wouldn't understand that I like having wild and adventurous sex."

Phillip's burning gaze moved downward to Baadar's crotch as he spoke, his voice dripping with innuendo.

"She is stronger than you realize, but you have made a mistake, Phillip, because you shouldn't have touched her. She's mine and mine alone now. I woke her from the sleeping curse." Baadar's voice echoed all around the room, then he bent down, bringing his face close to Phillip's. "So you like it when the witch pisses all over you, huh? Does that turn you on?"

Right. Baadar had mentioned something and I'd basically told him Phillip was into all kinds of forbidden fetish play. Now, the realization of what he'd done in the forest with the witch came to the forefront of my mind, which was totally what Baadar was aiming at with his boldness.

As Phillip inched closer to Baadar, my breath hitched. .

My pussy throbbed with desire as I watched them interact, the perfect balance of raw power and desperate need. As I thought about what was to come, I found myself unable to look away and even more determined to see through this enticingly forbidden scene.

"Kneel before me, Phillip!" Baadar demanded, his voice a deep rumble.

Without hesitation, Phillip obeyed, his eyes widening in awe as he took Baadar's huge erection in his hand.

My pussy begged for release so I circled my fingers around my clit. I should be jealous but this was all about power and dominance for Baadar—and that made me hot in all the intimate places.

"Open wide and take it all in," Baadar commanded. "I know you've been wanting this since I visited you in the cell."

With no further delay, Baadar thrust his large member into Phillip's mouth, causing a muffled moan to escape the prince's lips. I was too stunned to move or speak—all I could hear was Phillip's gagging as Baadar probed deeper into his throat. The monster growled with pleasure as Phillip grabbed his buttocks and pushed himself harder.

"Suck it, Phillip. Suck it hard. You are not Aurora so you don't have to worry about my monster emerging. He's tamed tonight but this feels fucking good." Baadar groaned when Phillip sped up the pace.

The sickening sight of Phillip struggling to contain Baadar's monstrous cock in his mouth should have repulsed me. Yet with each violent thrust, the heat of my arousal seeped through my clothes and pooled between my legs. I found myself for the monster's release so he could utterly consume Phillip and make him submit.

The freak didn't care about me—I'd always known deep down, yet I did my utmost to deny it. Now there was no doubt.

My fingers trembled as I slid them inside my panties, grazing the slick wetness that now flooded my folds. My monthly was at the tail end, so I felt clean and free.

If only it was me being pleasured by Baadar right now, me letting him consume me like a wild beast. I'd have given up all I could to be the recipient of his touch right now...

No, I wasn't jealous of Phillip. He didn't even stir the monster, so Baadar was simply toying with him like the barbarian he was.

Or toying with me, more like. Perhaps he wanted to scare me away. But I was no fool because I saw through the game he was playing.

More than recoil, I wanted to surrender to his will, to be his willing whore, slave to his ruthless domination.

Chapter Twelve

B aadar

Phillip's delicate lips wrapped around my cock. I wanted to finish inside his throat, feel him swallow every last drop of me. At the same time, I knew that Aurora was somewhere in the shadows, enjoying this scene that called to her darkest desires. She wanted me to punish Phillip and even though it seemed a bit cruel, I couldn't help but feel a thrill at her bravery and eagerness.

I put my hands behind my head and thrust my hips forward, serving my cock up to the hilt. He gagged and tears streamed down his face, yet I couldn't stop myself from feeling pleasure as he serviced me. Unsurprisingly, my monster was content with seeing another man submit to me and for a brief moment, I felt in control of this situation. But deep down, I was afraid that Aurora's feelings would be too strong for either of us to handle.

The princess was pleasuring herself, moaning with need. This woman was unbelievable. She was obviously turned on by what was happening and I was so impressed that she didn't lose her cool while she watched me engage in this scandalous act.

There were two ways this would go: she'd either steer clear of me for engaging in this tryst or see what a total dickhead Phillip was. I should want the first but honestly, the second would be so much more appealing.

In reality it was her I wanted to fuck, to fill with my seed and dominate the way I was doing with her prince. The orgasm built inside me just like that. My groin burned with raw fire.

"You're doing well, Prince Phillip, servicing your master like that. Now swallow my cum and don't you dare spill a drop."

As Phillip toiled away, I felt a mixture of emotions. His submissiveness gave me power over him, yet I knew this was wrong. He was so weak and removed from reality, yet still, he wanted to please me. As did Aurora.

My breathing became more labored as I neared the brink of release. I grabbed the back of his head, pushing him deeper onto my cock. My semen sprayed down his throat, draining me like my guilt.

Aurora fucked herself in earnest, desperate for something more as her heart stood on the verge of shattering. The pleasure was like an electric shock radiating through her body and I finally pulled out, gasping and scrambling for purchase, droplets of sweat clinging to my skin.

My sense of power started to ebb then. What had I done?

When I glanced at Phillip, he was on his knees before me, trembling, coated in my cum that dripped off his chin and throat. He was destroyed, utterly humiliated, degraded by my powerful dominance.

I grabbed his chin and tilted it up, so he couldn't avoid looking at me. Breaking him felt good, a just punishment—but Aurora? I could tell myself she deserved this too, but I'd be lying.

Despite my mixed feelings, her euphoria was palpable. I sensed no anger, no envy or dark thoughts. Her inner strength floored me. This proved to me once again that she was the one for me. If we mated, I bet she'd be the only woman ever who could handle my monster.

"Remember this lesson, Phillip. You're here to serve and obey me. This was only a gentle reminder that I own the princess so never, ever pull that stunt again. Now get the fuck out of here because I might change my mind and drown you," I barked.

In a flash he was back on his feet—weak but still hard, his body trembling. Then he picked up all his clothes and vanished before I could count to three.

Smiling to myself, I went back to the pool for a swim, wondering if the princess would be brave enough to leave her hideout and face me. I waited, hoping she would, but rather, she kept pleasuring herself. This woman was utterly foolish if she thought she would get away with this. I was planning to spank her hard, give her a lesson she would never forget. She needed to be punished for her deception.

After a long moment, I finally stepped up from the water and dried myself, then got dressed and left the washroom without so much as a glance her way. She was still frustrated, lost, and probably confused, but tomorrow would be a new day that would bring more opportunities to make her crazy with need for me.

She wanted me and I was planning to wait until

she asked me to mate with her, until she begged me to finally devour her body and soul.

Back in my chamber, I went to sleep without any issues, for the first time at peace with the world. No more guilt wracked me. I did what I had to. In the end, Aurora was mine and soon, our fate would be sealed.

* * *

"Where are we going?" Aurora asked the next morning.

She was riding with me again. We hadn't talked about what happened in the washroom because she kept pretending she hadn't seen me with her prince.

She shuddered when I wrapped my arms around her and pulled the reins to control the horse. I inhaled the scent of her morning arousal that filled me with life. My tentacles were ready to come out, but I took a few deep breaths to calm myself down. This wasn't the time or place.

"We are heading over to pay a visit to a certain demon. Once we have the firelight, the witch will know where to find us," I breathed into her ear, closing my eyes for a second to relish the scent of her.

Phillip rode in front of us with two of my men. We

had to be careful. We didn't want to bring too much attention to ourselves in this part of Moorhead. This whole territory teemed with wolfmen and cursed were-humans. They did not suffer trespassers.

"It's creepy here," Aurora said with a shudder. "Don't you leave me here to languish."

We journeyed on through the dense forest and it was hard to see more than a few feet in front of us. Phillip had been given thorough instructions from the warlocks about the demon's whereabouts and we were apprised on how to handle the magic, as well as any retaliation. But the creature had used the firelight to stay alive for centuries. He wasn't going to give it up easily.

Whatever happened, I had to protect the princess.

"We are stuck with each other, Aurora. Don't you remember the deal you made with me? You need to find that witch, too. She is the only one that can remove your curse," I reminded her.

She nodded but looked so thoughtful, I wondered what was on her mind. Tension was seeping out of her pores while my body instinctively reacted to her close-ness. my whole body was inflamed, because she was so close to me.

I glared at Phillip's back, my eyes glowing with a burning hatred. "If I go into heat soon then you and any female near me will be in grave danger," I said in a low voice. "So, I need to track down that witch so she can remove my monster curse as soon as possible. I don't want to put your life—or anyone else's—in unnecessary danger, Aurora."

I clenched the reins tight. Phillip looked back and caught me staring daggers. His normally cheerful expression was replaced with one of fear as he dismounted his beast. Knowing what was best for him, he turned away and ignored Aurora.

"I can handle you Baadar, so you don't have to be concerned," she said fiercely after I helped her get off the horse.

He should know I wasn't going to hurt him though. I needed him—for now. He had to be clever enough to know how to entice the demon and make some kind of deal with the witch if she showed. This was our only chance and everything needed to go according to plan.

I handed her a flask filled with water, not missing the trepidation in her eyes. I wished I could take away all her worries.

Everybody tethered their mounts to various trees and bushes. Shooting the prince a sharp look, she walked away. I frowned because she had no idea what she was getting into. She was not taking the situation seriously enough.

We set up camp and prepped for our encounter with the demon. The creature required a sacrifice, which was why we brought the lamb with us. This was one of the things the warlocks had told us about.

Two of my men slit the lamb's throat and drained its blood. The creature was brought to me and as I stared at it, at the life that had been sacrificed so I could be human again, I longed for what I once was. Finding the witch was crucial.

"Are we ready?" I asked, approaching Aurora and Phillip who were now standing close. Phillip had just told her something and she shook her head and turned away. Though they claimed their relationship was platonic, I couldn't help but feel a twinge of jealousy knowing that they had once been love interests. They shared a bond that made me question everything.

Phillip glared at Aurora, his voice charged with emotion as he spoke. "Yes we are ready, but I think the princess should stay behind. The mission's too dangerous."

The tension in the air was thick enough to touch and fear was a tangible entity that occupied the space. Even with the legendary stories of the demon swirling around, I had to trust in my abilities—this was just another monster that had chosen to live alone in the shadows. Tales said that he had been betrayed by a woman he loved and his heart was so scarred from her actions, he had locked away her virtue in an eternal fire which kept him alive.

This mystery might have been true, for surely a broken heart could turn anyone into a cruel, soulless demon.

"I won't need your protection, Phillip. Let's just get this over with," she said sternly as she entered the cave.

I followed her, feeling proud and yet dreading what was to come.

We left the rest of our party behind, Phillip cradling the lamb in his arms. As we stepped in the shadowy cave, I was overcome with an unfamiliar sense of longing and fear. I was scared of losing her and this was strange because I never thought I would care about anyone again.

All around us was silence, save for our own heavy breaths. My feet weighed me down with every step as though filled with lead. I couldn't bear the thought of anything happening to her, yet here we were, about to face one of the most dangerous monsters on Moorhead Mountain in order to steal the firelight from him.

We walked for about half an hour, following a narrow path until it finally widened.

"Look, it's a lake!" Aurora shouted, pointing at the water in front of us, Phillip placed the sacrificial lamb on the ground and approached the princess.

The energy in the air was oppressive, pressing down on us like a physical weight. The darkness shifted around us, like a menacing presence lurking in the shadows. My heart raced and my breath quickened, the taste of metal on my tongue almost like a warning. The silence was suddenly broken by the roar of bubbling water; the directionless vibration sounding like a beast's hunting call. I knew this was not going to be easy. Phillip acted like he could handle the demon, but that was a lie. I had to be ready to transform into my shadow self. A chill crept up my spine when I realized that something was coming our way.

A few moments later, a large creature arose from the lake and Aurora shrieked in terror. I was astounded by the power of the beast in front of me—he was three times larger than me and resembled a giant man with horns, bulging arms, and broad shoulders. His entire body was encased in scales and his glaring red eyes were fixed on Aurora.

"Ah, what have we here? The king himself,

presented before me to face his destiny," the demon thundered.

"We have a sacrifice for you. We have come to request the firelight to save lives and possibly, the kingdom," I announced, getting straight to the point. There was no reason to dwell on introductions. We had met in the past in different circumstances.

Water was dripping down the monster, over his enormous hairy torso. The smell of fresh blood and arousal was intense. Phillip looked pale and I wanted to punch him. He came along because he knew what to offer the demon. He assured me that the lamb would be enough.

"You are amusing me, Baadar. You think that a lamb filled with magic is going to be enough for me to hand over the firelight?" The demon laughed and his eyes shifted to Aurora. "She's going to be my sacrifice. I want her. She'll stay here with me and only then will I hand you the firelight."

Chapter Thirteen

urora

My grip on Phillip's arm tightened as fury and panic twisted inside me like a sharp blade. Baadar had lured me into this hellhole with his false promises of love, when in reality he just wanted to offer me as a sacrifice to this demonic entity.

I had trusted him, thought he'd finally seen my worth when he saved Phillip's life, but no ... he'd only wanted the prince for his own sick pleasure. Clearly, it had all been a ploy.

The realization of my own naivety knifed its way through my heart. Phillip's frightened eyes stared back at me and I knew I couldn't rely on him to get out of this. I was on my own.

"I'm afraid that's not an option. The princess belongs to me and she can't be your sacrifice. You must settle on the lamb!" Baadar roared, his powerful tentacles unfurling like whips. He swelled and shifted, turning into a gigantic beast, his tentacles lashing and weaving around Phillip and me. My heart thundered in my chest as I watched Phillip cower away, his face as white as a ghost's.

"I have been alone for a decade, and if you cared about the princess, Baadar, you wouldn't have brought her here," the demon spat, his eyes blazing like fire.

Baadar's menacing face seemed to contort in an expression of sorrow that I couldn't quite understand. The demon was right. He never cared about me—it was all just an illusion. He had been acting to gain my trust, possibly my love, but all as a means to an end. After all, he'd crowned himself king after stealing the kingdom. If he tied me to him and used Phillip like some sort of lapdog, there'd be nobody left to challenge his authority.

Disbelief and bitterness coiled around me as I came to terms with these horrible scenarios.

"You're right, Caveseeker. Take her as your sacrifice in exchange for the firelight!" Phillip spat out the words, his face twisted in rage. His icy gaze shot daggers into me as he pushed me away. My heart shattered like glass at the thought of being betrayed by the one I had once trusted the most. Baadar watched on with detachment, as if oblivious to my despair.

I stumbled backward, my breathing labored as I fought back tears. "How could you do this to me, Phillip?" I asked, aching for him to take back his words. But he only shook his head and stepped closer to the edge of the lake.

"I'm sorry, Aurora, but this has always been the plan. You in exchange for the firelight. The warlocks were clear on it," Phillip confessed with a sorrowful look.

Fury and sadness mixed together inside me. I stood with my fists clenched at my sides as I tried to make sense of it all. I wanted to laugh at how foolish I had been for believing either one of them would care about me.

Phillip smiled. "The king also agrees because he needs the firelight." Bile rose in my throat. I had no other choice but to accept my grim fate.

"I do need the firelight," Baadar agreed, and I swallowed.

The demon laughed, watching our exchange, then leaned closer to study me. My chest heaved and panic struck momentarily, followed by numbness. There was no escape for me. I'd walked right into this trap, not knowing what to expect.

The demon stared directly into my eyes, his face suddenly twisted in agony. "I have been waiting for this moment for centuries, my dearest princess," he said in a broken tone. "Ever since the woman I loved broke my heart beyond repair."

His words sunk like a dagger in my heart. All I could do was let silent tears fall.

"I'm sorry," Baadar interjected, his voice cracking as he faced me. "But I won't let you take Aurora away. You can have a part of my soul instead."

It took me a moment to understand what he was saying. Had he really offered himself up to save me? Tears spilled over my cheeks as the meaning of his words settled into my bones.

"What? Are you willing to sacrifice yourself for me?" I asked, feeling like my whole world had shifted beneath me.

"No Baadar, if you give him a part of yourself, the witch won't be able to break your monster curse!" Phillip shouted in a panic. "We have talked about it and we both agreed to give up Aurora!"

My heart dropped, the shock of betrayal causing me to stumble in the dark.

"Phillip, take Aurora away from here right now," Baadar commanded, and I lunged toward him.

"No!" I screamed as I grabbed at his tentacles. "You can't do this to yourself. You wanted to break the curse. Do you really want to be the tentacle monster forever?"

Baadar roared so loudly it shook the walls of the cave, and before I knew it Phillip had dragged me out of the lake, dragging me away from the tentacle monster through a narrow opening. I fought him tooth and nail—fists pounding and yells tearing out of my throat—but nothing mattered. Baadar had already made up his mind.

When he finally pulled me outside the cave, I tried to run back in and save Baadar, but Phillip held me back with all his might. I screamed and thrashed against him until my limbs shook with exhaustion. The world around me started to spin.

Baadar was not at all selfish and manipulative. He wasn't what I judged him so quickly to be—a traitor and ruthless traitor. He'd done this for me, out of pure love and caring—taking on the curse that had ruined his life. Tears streamed down my cheeks as I paced outside the cave, waiting for him to come out alive.

"How could you let him do this? How, Phillip? You're a fucking coward!" My voice seemed to reverberate through the forest. Taking advantage of a moment of distraction, I rushed inside the cave, as fast as my legs could take me, and found Baadar unconscious right inside the entrance.

"No!" I knelt next to Baadar, my despair crushing and debilitating. My fingers trembling, I touched his face, praying he was still alive.

"Tell me how to help him!" I begged.

Phillip stood next to me, his face drawn with exhaustion and guilt.

"Just let him rest. The witch should be here soon and she will heal him," he spoke softly.

Disbelief flooded me as I spun to face him.

"The witch. So if you know she's coming, you also know where she's been all this time?" I screeched.

He nodded solemnly and I turned away from him in disgust, rummaging through my bag, pulling out healing potions and flasks—anything that would help him recover. A wave of regret crashed against me as I realized what I had almost done—believing that Baadar intended to sacrifice me, when all he had ever done was protect me. And it was now too late for us because he'd sacrificed his humanity for me. He wouldn't allow another monster to take me, so desperate he was to protect me. I could tell by his pulse that he still lived, but he was a monster now and there would be no reversing it.

With tears streaming down my cheeks, I carefully poured the elixir into his mouth. Phillip had failed us both. Here I was being asked to accept that Baadar would remain a beast forever. As I prayed for some kind of miracle, I had to come to terms with the fact that this was the price of my freedom. My parents awaited me, and I was expected to become queen at some point. However, the thought of leaving Baadar behind forever felt like an insurmountable task.

"Aurora?" His voice reverberated through my body as I heard his plea. I hastily wiped the wetness from my cheeks and locked my gaze with his as I grabbed his hand and squeezed. He had to understand how devoted I was to him.

"What is wrong? I have been terrified of what could happen to you! Why would you put yourself in danger like that for me? There must be some explanation," I said, unable to quell the tears streaming down my face. His skin was feverish and the heat in his eyes told me all I needed to know.

So much had changed since I woke up that fateful day. I had foolishly thought he was nothing more than an unfeeling beast with tentacles, but I had come to discover there was far more to Baadar than his monstrous side. There was a person deep down, a worthy person ... a person who was mine.

"The demon has only taken the essence of my humanity. I will survive for a very long time. You don't have to pretend that you're worried about me, princess. Are those real tears?" he asked, lifting his hand and touching my cheek. I laughed and wiped the tears away. There was so much we needed to talk about.

"Yes, these are my tears, Baadar," I sobbed, no longer able to hide the powerful emotions that overwhelmed me. I sniffed. "What now? The witch can't break the curse?"

Phillip had vanished some time while the king's men surrounded us, fear and concern etched on their faces.

Baadar shut his eyes, a sad smile playing on his lips. "No matter what I do, this curse remains with me forever," he said, his voice laced with pain.

I grabbed his hand tightly as a barrage of new feelings assaulted me. We were not the same people anymore—something between us had shifted and we were inexorably changed in this moment. Phillip didn't matter now. He was nothing more than a distant memory.

I just wasn't ready to accept this. Maybe the last witch in Moorhead would find a way to help Baadar?

"Where is the fire magic? The witch might still help you. There must be a way for her to remove the curse," I said hopefully.

Baadar smiled. He was coming around, but still so weak. I gave him another potion, hoping he'd regain his strength quicker. We were away from his territory and he'd brought only a handful of men with him. These woods were filled with dangerous predators so this was going to be a challenge.

I had no idea what happened in that cave, but Baadar couldn't remain a tentacle monster forever.

One of his men brought him a clear flask with some liquid in it. I glanced around, searching for Phillip again, but he was gone. I had been ready to extend an olive branch and give him another chance but instead, he spat it all in my face. He'd been so ready to hand me over to the demon in the cave—no hesitation at all. I had a feeling he wouldn't show up ever again.

I lay down next to Baadar and he wrapped his arms around me. Maybe after all this, Baadar would take me back to my parents.

I had so many questions. Why had my father abandoned the crown, and me? Was he in hiding because of a threat? I had to find that blasted witch and figure all this out. But right now, all I could do was speculate. I wasn't ready to leave him just yet.

Soon we both drifted off to sleep, our future uncertain, but all was right with the world in this moment because I knew that the monster cared about me. He no longer wanted to kill me.

I didn't know how long we slept, but several hours later I was awakened by some strange noises. I lifted myself off the ground and stretched, listening to the moans and whimpers that came from the nearby forest. Baadar was still fast asleep and I shivered with the cold.

The sounds echoed off the trees, vibrating through my body. I peered around, straining to make out the source in the dead of night. Baadar's men were all asleep, and I realized that no one was guarding the camp. This wasn't ideal, especially if we were ambushed.

I flung a heavy blanket around me and ventured out towards the sound that now had intensified to labored panting. I kept walking until giggles filled the air, snapping me out of my thoughts. I maneuvered through the trees until darkness no longer obscured my vision.

Soon, I stepped around a huge bark and saw Phillip pinning a woman against a large tree, thrusting into her with vigor and urgency. He moved faster and faster, their bodies slamming together in a wave of passion.

"Phillip, darling, we aren't alone anymore," the dark-haired woman said, finally noticing me just standing there. I glanced away, embarrassed when the prince turned around to face me. I waited for him to pull his pants up before I stepped away. I had never seen the woman before and didn't recall her traveling with us.

"Aren't you going to introduce us, Phillip?" I asked then, emboldened. The bastard had more to be mortified about than I did.

"Aurora, this is Crystalia the witch who has come for the firelight," Phillip said, smoothing his hair. His eyes danced with amusement and pity. Idiot.

"The famous witch," I drawled, emphasizing her title. I was surprised how ordinary she looked or maybe it was just an illusion. Crystalia was the last witch of Moorhead, so she was very valuable to a lot of people. It seemed that she had a special relationship with Phillip.

"Well, well, well ... what a surprise," another voice made me jump. I turned around to see Baadar standing in the shadow of the moon. He was staring at the pair, his eyes gleaming dangerously. The potions must have given him the strength he needed to get back on his feet.

I wrapped the blanket tighter around me and swallowed hard, wondering if this whole thing could be sorted without any bloodshed.

Chapter Fourteen

Baadar

.

I could feel my heart racing as I stood in front of the witch, my body trembling as I remembered the pain she caused me all those years ago. The reflection of my cursed self reflected in her eyes—me, as I was—and I knew in that moment there was no hope of ever being set free.

I woke up alone earlier, feeling much more like myself again. The memories quickly flashed through my mind and I growled with frustration when I realized Aurora was not with me. On top of that, all my men were asleep, which put us in grave danger.

The demon from the cave craved her when she stood in front of him. He wanted to take her away from me, so I intervened. Only when I was just about to lose her I realized that I was in love with her. She was my mate, so I sacrificed myself instead. I did it to protect her and would do it all over again.

My primal nature took over then, my monster instincts leading the way as I tracked her scent beneath the silver light of the full moon. The air was heavy with her essence. Aurora was both terrified and aroused by my transformation. I had to protect her, no matter the cost.

As I crept closer, I spotted Phillip and the witch locked in a passionate embrace, their bodies entwined with celestial energy coursing between them like molten lava. Aurora must have just caught them screwing each other as the smell of sex lingered in the air.

I felt it rush through me too, igniting every bizarre cell in my being and replacing any lingering desires for revenge with a basic, primal need to mate.

Phillip's eyes met mine and he looked defeated, but his weakness was no longer attractive to me. Instead, I used him as a way to get closer to the princess. Aurora embraced my strength and dominance without knowing that it was built on Phillip's broken form. We were bound together by our carnal urges, ready to explore what neither of us had ever felt before. When the demon had taken my humanity, he made me go into heat, which complicated matters.

Crystalia's presence was like an electric shock coursing through my veins, stirring up long forgotten memories. Her wickedly seductive smile seemed to flicker in the dim light as she sauntered towards me. She had managed to retain her youth with her foreign magic. She had the power to remain hidden whenever she wanted, her head a heavy bounty on her shoulders.

"It's a real shame, isn't it, that you chose to follow the princess instead of staying true to your human form," she purred, tossing her hair back as her lips formed a dazzling smile.

Aurora was staring at her with a mixture of amazement and annoyance. I was shocked that the witch had picked Phillip out of all the men in Moorhead. He was a wimp and maybe that's what attracted her—the fact that she could dominate him so easily.

"Break Aurora's curse and leave before I hand you over to humans. We both know they will have your head and you won't be able to escape this time around.

There is a lot of blood on your hands, witch," I said, grabbing her wrist and pulling her to me.

She giggled, licking her lips as she threw a glance at the princess. Crystalia was resourceful and smart and that was why she was able to elude capture for so long.

Now though, this was her end. She couldn't get her hands on the firelight unless I handed it over to her. Only then would she become powerful enough to cling to her youth forever.

I made my decision earlier on and sacrificed my humanity for the woman I was supposed to hate and yet loved.

Aurora stepped next to me, her eyes filled with unholy anger as she stared at Crystalia.

"Why did you curse me? Who made you do it?" Aurora asked, her voice high and loud in the vast, otherwise silent space. That was a good question, and one I had been avoiding for years. I had no idea what had happened after I left Moorhead, but I knew that it had something to do with her father.

"Aurora, that was years ago," Phillip interjected softly. "Trust me, you don't need these answers."

I shook my head. "Let her talk. We all need answers," I said firmly. I was treading on thin ice because asking too many questions could lead her to discovering uncomfortable truths.

But Aurora deserved to know the truth, whatever that entailed.

"I'll ask you again, why did you curse me and who made you do it?" the princess repeated.

"I want to tell you the truth, Princess Aurora, but I am bound by a powerful magic that prevents me from disclosing it," the witch said, her smile fading.

Aurora breathed heavily and her scent intensified, but I could also feel something else. Something stirred deep inside of me—my monster was about to come out.

"Then defy this curse and tell me what you know," Aurora demanded, glancing at Phillip. "Do you know who cursed me?"

But before he could answer, I let out a deafening roar and lost control of my beast. The monster was ready to emerge and claim his mate. This was happening way too fast, but I couldn't control the urge that spread through my body.

"You better run, Aurora. The tentacle monster has just lost control... You are free of the sleeping curse, but not free of his tentacles," I heard Crystalia say to Aurora before hell broke loose.

The witch grabbed the prince's hand and they vanished in a puff of smoke. I spread my arms and roared, the sound echoing in every corner of the forest.

Aurora shrank away from me, her eyes wide with fear. My arms had lengthened into tendrils, writhing and curling around me in rage. The tentacles started to grow as the transformation began.

"Run, my princess. Listen to the witch. Run as fast as you can!" I shouted, my body shaking with the force of my hunger.

Aurora stumbled backwards then turned to flee. I watched her disappear, relieved that she had the sense to get away before I could do her any harm.

For a while, even before I arrived to wake her up from the sleeping curse, I thought I could avoid this, that I would never have to hurt another female, but it was too late. The demon from the cave had triggered all of this.

All of my worst nightmares were coming alive for there was no way to escape the monster within. Heat rushed through my veins, my muscles thickened and bulged as my joints shifted.

My skin felt like it was being seared from the inside out, and a blaze of ashen fire emerged from my every pore. With every step I took, I was closer to embracing my dark side.

I ached for the female, an invisible force compelling me ever closer. Her scent saturated my senses, her presence enveloping me in a primal frenzy. I became obsessed with her, my hunger for her body driving me mad. My tentacles quivered in anticipation as I spied her entering an old barn on the edge of the forest. The desire to consume her gripped me, sharpening my senses and heightening my emotions beyond control.

A wolf's howl in the distance only served to fuel my rage. The very air around me hummed with Aurora's essence. I advanced through the trees with a feral ferocity, tracking the woman who had so effortlessly captured my heart. She was to be my mate, my woman, and the mother of my children.

Adrenaline surged through my veins as I stepped into the shadows of the forest, my whole body becoming one with the monster I had become.

My movements were precise and calculated, but my mind raced with excitement—I had found her. She belonged to me, my precious possession that I craved and desired. With every breath, I tasted her sweet scent, feeling it linger on my skin like a warm blanket. Nothing else mattered in that moment. I was completely and utterly alive.

I slowly advanced toward the old barn, my tentacles quivering in anticipation. I knew she was waiting there, moving past her fear by readying herself to succumb to the punishment I was about to inflict on her for running away from me.

True, I was the one who asked her to do that, but none of it mattered. A faint whisper of my past self told me not to hurt her, that she wasn't like all the other women I'd been with before. She was the forbidden fruit, the untouchable princess I was never supposed to lay a hand on. But I couldn't listen.

I shoved open the doors and saw her cowering in the corner, straw piled up around her. The animals had been gone for years and she was the only living thing in her. Her heart was beating erratically and her body brimmed with arousal, but I knew that by the end of the night, she would be begging me to set her free.

"Come out, come out wherever you are, princess. Your king is here, your mate and your master!" I roared, breathing hard. I was completely lucid, but filled with vicious desire and need to consume her body until she begged me to stop. My tentacles spread further and my cock was hard.

Longing for her filled my veins like fire, burning through me. Each time I tried to suppress these feelings, they only seemed to grow stronger. Until tonight, when I could no longer resist the overwhelming cravings and need that coursed through me. It was like a wildfire of emotion that threatened to consume me utterly.

"I'm here, Baadar, and I'm not afraid because I

consent to be your mate," she said, coming out of hiding. Fresh determination showed on her face, and she glowed with confidence and power. I let go of a growl as my tentacles danced around me. Then, I removed my shirt and tossed it aside.

"Take off your clothing and come to me, Aurora," I growled, my blood pounding with primal lust.

She tilted her head to the side and smiled, a wicked glint in her eye, before slowly peeling away her clothing. As each item hit the floor, my heart rate increased, and I felt my muscles tense with carnal anticipation.

I was so tempted to overpower her, to make her beg for my touch, yet somehow, to my surprise, I was able to restrain myself. I wanted to savor this moment of power and control over her body, for there was something different and intensely thrilling about it. Soon, she stood before me in nothing but her own skin, a vulnerable yet tantalizing offering.

"What are you going to do to me, my king? I have been mischievous because I was touching myself while I was waiting for you to come to me," she said, bringing her hand to her lips and licking it.

Why was she enticing my monster further? Didn't she know what she was playing with?

I parted my lips and emitted a loud curse. This was the most erotic image I had ever seen and she was mine.

My whole body reacted, my skin itched for contact, and the monster inside me turned feral. A split second later, I had her in my arms. I fisted her hair and pulled.

"My monster has crawled out of the depths of my soul and it's ready to ravage you," I hissed, seeing the anticipation in her eyes before crashing my lips onto hers.

I kissed her with an intensity that could only come from being deprived of happiness and finding myself trapped in the addicting lure of her scent. Our tongues intertwined as if they were one, and we devoured each other. She tasted like honey and vanilla, like a sweet nectar made just for me.

Our bodies moved in perfect harmony until my mouth roved down her neck, licking and suckling her skin as she moaned in pleasure. My fingers tugged and pulled on her hair as I trailed kisses along her collarbone.

"Baadar, this feels incredible," she gasped as my lips engulfed her hardened nipple, sending electric shocks through her body. My tentacles were begging to be allowed to join in the fun, but first I wanted to taste how sweetly aroused she was. Her breathing was ragged, there was no doubt her womanhood was drenched from desire.

"Are you ready to come for me like a good girl if I

keep pleasuring your nipples, princess?" I snarled, sliding my fingers through her sopping wetness. Her breaths came in short, desperate gasps as I grabbed her hips and tugged them closer to mine.

"I want you to make me yours. Unleash your power..." she moaned, her eyes shut tight as she begged for more.

I could feel her body trembling in anticipation. Grinning wickedly, I reached out and embraced her with my tentacles. One slipped between the crack of her ass cheeks and the other smacked her pussy hard. She screamed in ecstasy, her eyes wide with raw pleasure.

"Kneel before me, princess," I commanded, and my tentacles pried her legs apart, forcing her onto her knees. She gasped, desperate to touch herself, but I would not let her. She would have to earn her pleasure, for that was what my mighty form demanded.

I yanked my pants down and freed my manhood, stroking it in my hand as the princess stared in unbridled lust. She'd never be able to fit me in her mouth. I was more immense than the average man, and today I was even bigger than usual. But oh, how she desired it. She was already licking her lips, wanting me to shove it in her mouth so I could dominate and degrade her like a whore.

"Tap my leg if it becomes too much for you to bear, princess," I said, pulling hard on her hair then thrusting my cock between her lips. Such exhilaration surged through me at her muffled cries—she was struggling to fit me in! "You're so brave, princess, trying so hard to please me. Suck it like a good girl."

I wouldn't last long—two of my tentacles had already begun to slither between her legs and brush against her pulsating pussy. I closed my eyes and clutched her face as I thrust into her mouth with all the strength I could muster. It was unbearable for her, but her pussy dripped with arousal—she loved being taken by me.

This would be a long night of domination and she had no idea what was yet to come.

Chapter Fifteen

 urora

Desire thrummed through me as his immense cock filled my mouth. I gasped and my jaw quivered from the strain of being filled so completely.

His relentless rhythm sent shockwaves of pleasure through me and my jaw ached while tears spilled from my eyes. I wanted more, even though I was full to the point of gagging.

Out of the blue, a tentacle stroked my pussy and I let out an ecstatic moan when another nuzzled against my clit. A wave of pleasure crashed over me.

My body was aroused beyond belief and I could feel a sensational orgasm building inside me.

"Such a good girl... now let me come all over your perfect breasts, princess," he growled desperately and his words sent a shockwave of pleasure through me.

His movements were driving me insane and making me gag, yet I craved every touch. My mind was spinning, overwhelmed by the incredible sensations as he thrust his cock into my mouth. Crying out with pleasure, he pulled out and I felt his hot release all over my chest and face. I shuddered uncontrollably as his tentacles explored my body, pushing me to the brink of madness.

Then it all stopped and I cried out when he removed his tentacles and laid me down on the straw.

"Princess, I think you deserve all the rewards for sucking my cock so well, I can't wait to fill your tight. throbbing cunt with my cock and my tentacles. This is going to be a long night and I don't think you're ready for what's coming," he said as his tentacles were lifting me off the ground.

I begged Baadar for release, pled for him to give in to his hunger and let me shatter in bliss. My voice was unrecognizable, distorted by desperation.

"Oh, princess," he uttered, regret tingeing his voice as his tentacles circled my body, "I want to devour your tightness. I want to drown in your desire. But I must hold back. I can't risk my monster's wrath. It's a fine line."

His tentacles lifted me off the ground and I remembered again the sensation of them sliding around my thighs in the washroom. Suddenly, my pussy was in front of his face and I felt my legs being spread wide. I was so close now, a few licks away from climax. The intensity of it was too much to bear.

"Just do it already," I panted, ready to beg over and over.

I gasped in raw anticipation as he moved closer, his lips then fixating on my clit. His powerful suction sent fire coursing through me, electrifying my core as his tongue slid deep inside me. I was overwhelmed by the sudden onslaught of pleasure and my muscles tensed in response while screams spilled out of my mouth in a frenzy. I could only hope that we were far enough to prevent any curious villagers from coming to investigate the source of this noise.

My entire body trembled in mounting ecstasy as every nerve lit up with an electric pleasure, racing through me while his tentacles expertly massaged my nipples and clit. I couldn't tell how long I was suspended in a state of bliss, but by the time it ended, I was completely spent.

My chest heaved and my muscles refused to relax while his tentacles kept their hold of me.

"You're so beautiful, Aurora, and all mine," he said as he laid me down and soothed me with gentle caresses. "I can't wait to be finally inside you, but you need to sleep."

His words dragged me slowly into a deep slumber despite the protests of my body.

In the morning, I was awakened by the chirping of the birds. I was lying on the straw entangled with a warm body of muscles and tentacles, slippery and wet things all around my thighs and back. I opened my eyes, inhaling the scent of sex and sweat. Wide blue eyes were staring down at me. The king was so handsome and I wondered if he was in control of himself in this moment. I blushed a little, remembering last night and all the pleasure he'd given me, over and over.

"How are you feeling, princess?" he growled, pressing his lips savagely against mine.

I felt every inch of him and my body coursing with desire even as my jaw ached from last night's ecstasy. I needed his dominance and power as much as I craved for another rush of pleasure that only he could give me. I knew he was only just getting started.

"Good, relaxed and ready for more," I panted, my heart racing in anticipation.

His eyes glowed with the fire of a thousand demons and a sinister smirk spread across his handsome face. He was so unbelievably beautiful, even as a beast. With his tentacle writhing around us, he still radiated humanity. My soul screamed for him, wild and unhinged.

"You don't stop surprising me, my Aurora. I want to fuck you with all my tentacles, to fill your every hole until you beg me to stop," he said, and then one of his tentacles moved between my legs, sliding over the crack of my ass.

I shuddered, so very wet and needy again. Anticipation gripped me and my nipples hardened when his erection pressed against my center.

"Do it, don't hesitate—I'm ready for you so just fuck me already," I said, biting my lower lip. I knew I could handle his intensity, the punishment and the pain.

"As you wish, my princess," he growled.

In an instant his wet tentacles moved quickly and bound my thighs. I yelped in surprise when one squeezed my nipple while the other spanked my pussy.

I quivered from the intense burning sensation that shot through my body. Soon I was on all fours, unable to move as his tentacles entwined around me.

"Aurora, you look so delicious and I can't wait to slip my cock into your pussy. Last night you made a hell of a mess. I want to breed you. I want to possess you," he said, caressing my backside. His words called to my inner wanton. "How does that feel?"

His tentacles ripped through my thighs, sending a shiver of anticipation up my spine that settled deep in my belly. I felt a sharp pain when his slimy arms massaged my breasts and squeezed them tight, his fingers like razor-sharp claws digging into my flesh.

I groaned, trying to suppress the pleasure that rose within me like wildfire. I had wanted this for so long, and now I was finally giving in to it. His monster had me completely under its control, and before I knew it he had slapped my ass twice harshly, causing me to scream out in pain. The pain and pleasure were intertwined, dizzying my mind and setting my skin ablaze.

He said his monster could kill a feeling, but all I felt was ecstasy.

"Your arousal is intoxicating," he growled, and with one more slap of his tentacle on my pussy, I could no longer bear it. The intense torture left me sobbing. He caught me by the hips, admiring the burning skin as I lay there trembling and desperate in his arms. The warmth from his touch was like a drug and it filled every corner of my being until finally, I felt the liquid pleasure spilling from me. My heart raced in my chest as if it would burst any second.

"Why is there so much liquid?" I asked, ready to come just from all that stimulation. His tentacles were suddenly everywhere, squeezing my breasts, stimulating my clit, and pinching my nipples.

"So you can take two at the same time," he whispered in my ear. Then, without preamble, he thrust his hard erection into me. He was huge, massive, and I wasn't ready. "Fuck, princess, you feel better than I expected. So fucking tight, soaking and prefect."

He fucked me hard and fast while I cried, crying unable to comprehend what was happening. His cock felt like he was splitting me in half and I loved it. I came again and again as he continued to ravage me with his massive cock.

His slimy, sticky tentacles were everywhere and when I opened my eyes, I was suddenly on my back. I stared at the monster who was taking me as he wanted —violently, brutally, and from every possible position.

My body trembled with pleasure as his tentacles dug into my nipples. His wet suction felt like an electric current, sending me over the edge with orgasm after orgasm. I screamed out in passionate abandonment as he filled me with his hot seed, while his powerful arms pinned me down so hard, I thought my bones would break.

I loved it all and through the storm, he stared at me in wonderment.

I'd never experienced anything so intense before, but by that point I was past caring if he hurt me. All I wanted was more of him—his scent, his touch, and his teasing lips that drove me wild with pleasure and pain.

It was a dizzying sensation that blurred the boundaries between ecstasy and agony.

His hot breath tickled my ear as his monstrous words echoed between us. "My beast demands your ass, princess. I want to double-penetrate you."

Arousal flooded through me, sending a shiver down my spine despite the exhaustion that had taken over my body. I didn't know how long we had been locked in this barn, exploring each other with wild and explosive orgasms that had become our sustenance.

I was suddenly hesitant, afraid of the unknown depths he had taken me to and back again. But still I wanted him. I wanted all of him inside of me. His tentacles covered me like a blanket as his words sent a wave of heat crashing through my core.

"Will it hurt?" I asked, knowing full well that I

would do anything for him. He paused for a fraction of a second before whispering back, "It will be worth it. I'm amazed at how you took my cock..."

Yet, even while he spoke, a flash of uncertainty tinged his gaze.

Still, there was no going back now.

My body shuddered as he pushed me beyond my comfort zone into a realm of pleasure unlike anything I had ever known.

"Come here and lie over me so your pussy is on my face and you can play with my balls at the same time," he commanded.

I complied, feeling his lips on my wetness, his tongue flicking over my clit as his hands held my ass cheeks in a firm grip. Pleasure rioted through me when his smaller tentacle began to rub against my tight rear hole.

The sensation was intense, and Baadar moaned in approval when his tentacle released a sweet liquid that sent my body into overdrive. My mouth ached so much. I choked on his hard cock while his two tentacles simultaneously drove into me, pushing me to a dizzying climax.

"So fucking sweet. Break apart for me, darling. Your ass feels so good. I'm going to fuck you so hard you won't be able to walk for days," he murmured as he sucked on my clit with furious hunger. I shook in ecstasy as both tentacles penetrated me in perfect synchronization—one passionately thrusting into my ass while the other owned my pussy.

"Harder!" I demanded, my body quivering in ecstasy as yet another orgasm convulsed through me. I screamed his name and he continued to ravage me, pushing me further and further past any limit I'd ever known. His tentacles pounded into both of my holes simultaneously, and I felt myself being broken apart, my entire world turned upside down by his passionate assault. Still, I wanted more.

"More... yes! Take it, my king. Take all of it."

"Aurora ... I cannot believe this. You're amazing..."

I was covered with his sticky semen, my pussy was throbbing, and I was lost, fucked and completely split into pieces.

Then he suddenly changed position and placed me on top of him while I struggled to catch my breath.

He was unbelievable, rough and raw. This was the real tentacle monster, the man who'd awakened me in every sense of the word.

"Maybe it's because you're my mate. You're destined to be mine. You *are* mine..." he whispered, wide-eyed. So many emotions simmered in his beautiful eyes. "I love you, Aurora. This stands against everything I have ever believed or expected, but I am utterly yours. And you're here, safe, wanting my monster, unhurt by my monster..." His voice broke at the end.

I couldn't answer because my heart was so filled with happiness. I bent down and cradled his face, telling him with my expression and actions how I felt for him, pouring all my emotions in a gentle kiss.

Because I knew then that I was in love with him, too—even though a tiny voice inside my head insisted on reminding me that this could never work.

Chapter Sixteen

B aadar

I couldn't get enough of her and over the next three days, I fucked Aurora as often as I could, until she was too sore to move. In the end, she begged me to give her rest and I wouldn't. She came again and again, in earth-shattering screams of pleasure. Finally, after three days of no sleep and constant fucking, my body returned to its normal form, and I collapsed into a deep sleep on top of her. When I awoke, she was gone, probably sick of me by then. I chuckled at the thought.

She'd survived me. Survived the dreaded heat.

Aurora had made it through the mating ritual

alive, and I was both relieved and terrified. On the one hand, I was so happy that I hadn't hurt her during the ritual, but on the other hand, I was scared of what would happen when she learned the truth about my royal bloodline. I had been born with the birthright to rule this kingdom, but with that came a lot of responsibility I wasn't sure I was ready for.

"We need to stop at the nearest tavern and get you a proper meal. You must be starving. We have been here for days," I said when she sat in front of me on the horse.

I had tried so hard to deny it, but I could no longer ignore the fact that I would remain a monster forever. This was my destiny, and it had shaped me into whatever I was today. I accepted the fact that Aurora might bear me children with tentacles, but at the same time, I was afraid that she might never understand my choices.

"Yes, I am pretty hungry but don't worry, your tentacles were keeping me filled," she joked, unaware of the dark truth I was about to lay out in front of her.

"Do you still see yourself with me in the future?" I asked nervously, thinking about the fate of our relationship once she discovered what had happened to her father and mother.

The ride to the tavern was short and there were a

lot more people inside than I expected. The tower was at least a day's ride from here and I was certain my men had already returned safely.

At the same time, I had no idea what had happened to the prince and the witch. They both had the firelight now. I wouldn't be surprised if Crystalia had ditched the prince since she already got what she wanted.

We entered the tavern and all eyes were instantly on us. They recognized me. I asked for drinks and food for both of us and the innkeeper went out of his way to make sure we were both satisfied. When Aurora was eating, people openly stared. Nothing I could do about that.

"I care for you, Baadar, and I share your feelings but I need to see about my parents. I'm sure my father is still out there, looking for me," she said, taking a sip of her wine and staring at me with her expressive green eyes.

I had been expecting this conversation for so long, yet now I wasn't sure what to say.

"Then we must travel to find them. It's time," I replied reluctantly, even though the rational part of my mind reminded me that this was a bad decision. Her father had wronged us both and no amount of vengeance could make up for that.

Her eyes lit up and my heart sank with guilt. I didn't want to make her unhappy, but it seemed that the only way to keep her safe was to stay away from them.

Before we got back on the road, the tavern keeper wished us safe travels and told us to watch out for wolfmen. After we returned to the tower, we'd rest for a few days and then I'd set out with Aurora. I did not look forward to the encounter with her father, but this was inevitable.

Around a half mile later, we had to stop because Aurora was feeling nauseous, so she went into the bushes. I sat down on a log and contemplated the past. I hated myself for being fueled by revenge for so long. Now, I'd finally come to terms with things and I was at peace with myself.

At the same time, I wasn't sure if I was ready to fully give up. The demon had taken my humanity away, so now I was going to remain a monster forever. Whether she wanted to or not, Aurora was the cause of it. In truth, her entire family was the bane of my existence. Yet, now she was a part of me. My true mate.

I gave in to sleep at last, my eyes heavy and my body ready to drift away. There was something wrong, some nagging feeling, but I didn't want to face it so I succumbed to the darkness.

Suddenly, a loud cry and someone pushing me brutally jolted me back to reality.

How much time had passed? Minutes or hours? I couldn't tell, but the metallic taste in my mouth told me I had been poisoned. In that moment, I wanted nothing more than to unleash my beast and teach those responsible a lesson. But then I saw Aurora, her eyes wide with terror, and I froze for a moment. Thankfully, she wasn't hurt.

"He's not going to hurt you, Father! What is it that you hope to gain by imprisoning him?" she said, pleading with her eyes and voice.

I glanced around at the handful of men surrounding us, realizing we had been caught in a trap orchestrated by the man I had been wishing to destroy for many years: Aurora's father.

Although he had aged since the last time I saw him, his presence still commanded respect. His silver hair and beard framed green eyes so much like Aurora's, and his patrician nose gave him an air of nobility.

"Well, well, well, who do we have here? The monster in his human form," Stefan sneered as he spoke.

"How did you manage to track us down to the tavern and pay some poor soul to slip a potion in our food?" I asked, avoiding Aurora's gaze. She still had no idea what was happening and that was probably for the best. His smirk indicated he had been planning this for some time.

"Nobody can buy loyalty like the right bestowed on me," he replied with a wicked glint in his eye.

Rage coursed through my veins as I watched him stand in front of Aurora, his men blocking her path with their swords. I wanted to tear them apart, to rip off their hands and make them suffer. I had let down my guard for an instant, underestimating Stefan and his powers. Now I regretted not finishing him off years ago when I had the chance.

His face whitened though as he tried to make sense of the situation. Aurora loved me—it was clear as day from her words and actions—and as I predicted, he couldn't stand it.

"He's a monster, Aurora. Did he hurt you?" he demanded, adjusting his grip on the blade that burned with his magic. The energy was wearing off but not quickly enough. Now I was at his mercy.

Aurora's cheeks turned pink and she threw me a brief glance. So many unspoken words hung in the air between us. She understood how much I had sacrificed for her, how I had broken an ancient curse to save her life.

"Father, he hasn't hurt me. He broke the curse

before Phillip even had a chance and now I love him. He saved my life and gave up his humanity to do it," she said, standing unfazed in the face of Stefan's rage.

Her father stood to his full height, his face a mask of rage as the veins in his neck started to bulge and quiver with an intensity that was palpable. His entire body seemed to pulse with the sheer force of his anger, the energy radiating outwards like heat waves. Nothing had changed—Stefan still hated me and I was going to savor this moment forever. It was, after all, what I wanted.

"Aurora, you know nothing," Stefan seethed, allowing his rage to consume him. "You have failed me! I have tried to shield you from my brother for all these years, yet here we are. He has tricked you into believing that he cares for you. However, he has never shown any love for anyone but himself," he spat, his voice quaking with unbridled fury.

"Do not listen to his lies, Aurora! I have never used you and the love I feel for you is true," I roared.

"Hang on... Brother? What makes you think Baadar is related to you?" Aurora asked in bewilderment, and a wave of shame washed through me. All this time I had been keeping this secret from her... I should have revealed the truth long ago.

"Your father is my stepbrother, Aurora," I said

reluctantly, not wanting to reveal this particular truth at this time. I could see the pain wash over her face and it caused a deep ache in my heart. "My mother was the queen after her husband died, leaving a son that she loved like her own—me. I was so young at the time, I barely remember. She married your grandfather after his wife died childless, then had your father, who over the years would never accept that I was the true king. That's why he got Crystalia to curse me all those years ago."

I had never truly desired to have this crown, but when the choice had been taken away from me and Stefan took matters into his own hands, I fought for it.

Aurora frowned as she processed what I'd just told her. We were not related by blood, and it was only happenstance that I'd be considered her uncle. After a few moments, a gasp escaped her and she shot a piercing gaze at her father, her expression filled with betrayal and disbelief.

"This is impossible. My father is the only legitimate king! He wouldn't do something like that, wouldn't you, Father?" she said, her voice riddled with shock and confusion.

"My father was a fool, he never knew how to rule," Stefan spat out, a cruel smirk playing on his lips. "He was so besotted with his new wife, he would give the kingdom to a boy who wasn't even his blood. The queen might have ruled before him, but she wasn't really interested in politics, anyway."

My anger boiled up inside me and I growled with rage. All I wanted to do was reach out and snap his neck right then and there, but the magic prevented my transformation. I never looked at Aurora as my niece. I searched for her to kill her, to seek revenge, but instead I'd fallen in love with her.

"The woman that you later murdered in cold blood!" I roared with rage. "After your father passed, you wanted her out of the way so you could take what wasn't yours to begin with! Too bad that I managed to survive what came after. I returned to claim the throne and that's when you cursed me. You turned me into a monster, hoping this would take care of the problem."

Aurora shook her head. This was too much for her to wrap her head around, but I owed her the truth.

"Your stepbrother is Baadar and you never even once mentioned it. I can't believe this ... I can't believe that both of you kept this from me," she whispered.

"I love you, Aurora and the fact that you were Stefan's daughter never mattered to me. I have been searching for you all this time and when I finally found you, I couldn't bring myself to hurt you..."

"He's a beast, my dear daughter, and his own

mother was a whore. He did not deserve to be king," Stefan spat.

"Let him go right away, Father! You have lied to me for years!" she shouted as she broke down in tears. My heart was breaking to pieces. I hated seeing her so hurt and disappointed. "Tell me, *uncle*, has it been your plan all along to seduce me for revenge, then kill me? Because you wanted to get back at my father?"

Uncle—she spat the word at me and her eyes filled with a venomous rage that wracked me to the core.

The silence seemed to thicken around us, and Stefan grinned. He was getting what he wanted— isolating me and making Aurora hate me. It was my fault for not saying the truth. Now it was too late.

"Yes, I wanted revenge at first, Aurora. Your father had kept me away from his family and the court all your life and then destroyed me. He also murdered the woman I loved, Lilith, and cursed me into becoming a monster," I replied in a surprisingly even tone. "But then I kissed you and you woke up, and I was done for. It didn't take long for me to fall in love with you."

"Enough!" Stefan bellowed, signaling his soldiers to move forward.

"No! Father, you will not harm him," Aurora declared, stepping in front of me. "I am still your only daughter, destined to be the Queen of Moorhead, and you have been foolishly hiding all this time. You abandoned your kingdom. Baadar won't come after you. I promise you that, Father, but this must stop. The damage has been done and I won't take any more of this unnecessary bloodshed." She turned to me and continued, "Lead me to my mother so I can take some time to process what has happened."

"If he lives, he will keep coming after us," Stefan warned coldly, locking eyes with me. Aurora shook her head, then turned to face me. My heart was jackhammering inside my chest. She was furious with me and this was all my fault.

"He won't let this go," Vlad hissed menacingly, pinning me with a lethal glare.

Aurora shook her head in disbelief, then turned to face me with wild fury in her eyes. My heart pounded like a jackhammer inside my chest. She was furious with me and I deserved all her loathing.

"If you ever loved me ... because this is what you claim ... then you will leave us alone and let me take the crown. Only one monarch can rule over Moorhead, *Uncle*, and my father is obviously not fit for purpose," she shot him a fleeting glare, "so the kingdom belongs to me, the Queen," she spat in a tone as cold as ice.

I wanted to rip Stefan's heart out and then force it back through his throat. He had turned Aurora against me and I could never forgive him for it. I bared my teeth in a feral snarl even though what I wanted most was to talk to her, to apologize and show her how much I cared. She needed to understand that I had never meant to hurt her, that I still loved her beyond anything.

Most importantly, I was no blood relation.

"I do love you and I obey your wishes, Aurora. I won't come after your father again. My revenge is a thing of the past now," I growled out after a long moment.

Stefan stared at me with pure hate. He had no excuse to just kill me like he had planned.

"Let's take our leave, Father," Aurora said mechanically. I wanted to cry out to her to stop, I couldn't let her go like this.

She couldn't just throw away everything we'd been through.

"The potions should fade soon enough, brother. I think we are finally even," Stefan murmured darkly, lightly patting me on the shoulder. "You will never have her."

urora

A few days later

Somewhere in Moorhead

It had been too long since I had last seen my parents, and I never imagined that my life would take such twists and turns. But here I was, trudging through the castle walls, back to the place where I had lived with my father so long ago. As I arrived at my chambers, he dropped the bomb that ripped through my soul: my beloved mother was gone, drowned in a vicious storm which had swallowed up the ship she was sailing on three years prior.

My father's dream of reclaiming his kingdom had been a goal of his for years, and despite what I'd said about him not being fit for purpose, he kept claiming he was finally able to take back the crown when he returned to Moorhead.

As for me, I was too tired to argue.

Too broken to protest.

All the while I stayed tucked away in my chambers, trying desperately to make sense of it all. I hardly slept for three days straight, for thoughts of Baadar ran through my mind every second of every hour as I struggled with grief and pain.

Despite not being related by blood in any manner, he was still what the world would view as my step uncle, my forbidden lover—a mistake I had come to regret. I had been foolish to think that our union would go unchallenged, but still I found it hard to accept my father's bitterness towards Baadar.

When I finally came to my senses, I went to my father and laid out the future for him. I would be queen and there was nothing he could do about it. If he fought me, I'd make sure the people of the kingdom would learn about his scheming. I dared him to hurt me like he'd done his brother, and I knew he wouldn't because as twisted and evil as he was, he drew the line at harming his own daughter.

After all, he'd always told me I was his weakness.

While tomorrow marked the day of my coronation as queen, I felt betrayed by the lies my father had kept from me. How could he have kept Baadar's existence a secret? How could he have done the things he did?

My heart suffocated with the sheer betrayal of it all. Especially when it came to Baadar. He claimed to love me yet he'd used me, keeping secrets for his own ends. He had duped me and that was something I could never forgive. Now all I felt was pain, while I was fated to take up the mantle of ruler of Moorhead and face an uncertain future.

Tomorrow I would receive the crown, a reward for the breaking of my sleeping curse. But I still wasn't sure how I felt about it. Baadar had never said he was going to step down as king, and I still longed for him as much as I longed for my freedom. My father also wanted me to marry Phillip as originally intended, the prince who had gone missing, along with the mysterious witch. Yet I didn't care what happened to him after the way he had tried to hand me over to the demon.

I was all kinds of fucked up.

I sighed heavily and glanced at the clock. It was late in the evening, after the witching hour, and I knew sleep would not come easily. So I decided to go for a walk around the palace. I grabbed my blade and slid it in my boot. After what happened in the forest, I never ventured out without a weapon. I was in the palace where I belonged, but I noticed that people were still suspicious of me. I was leery of trusting anyone. It wasn't like I was such a great judge of character, so I couldn't let my guard down.

I was going to be queen and I didn't have a consort, so I had to work twice as hard to gain the respect of the people around me. Now, after all these years, I was finally free of the sleeping curse and back in my ancestral home.

I knew my father had used Crystalia to curse Baadar, but why had she cursed me? She'd said she was bound by magic and even if she could, she couldn't reveal the reason why.

I left my chamber and started walking toward the library. Several lords resided in the castle now and although this place had been my home, it now felt foreign in many respects. This was going to be a long and hard transition.

Baadar ... what was I going to do about him? Many

of these people now knew him as the king. Now I walked up here, for all intents and purposes a stranger, and everything was changing again.

But how could I forgive all the lies?

At the same time, he mated with me and I found myself unable to sever the connection. Thoughts of Baadar haunted me day and night. Since I was now expected to choose a husband, I felt sick to the stomach at the notion. Because I couldn't belong to anyone else—ever.

I walked in silence toward the library. It was so quiet, and I loved how the palace was deserted at this hour.

My mind wandered off to the night in the temple when I saw Baadar with the prince. My cheeks flushed when I thought about how much I was ready to take Phillip's place back then. How aroused I'd been.

All of a sudden I stopped in my tracks when I heard voices coming from my right. I hid behind a pillar, wondering who else wasn't sleeping. For a split second, I was ready to announce my presence because I recognized my father's hair in the dim light, but then I saw he wasn't alone.

"I have been waiting for this moment for so long," an unfamiliar voice said. I frowned, finally able to see a woman. She was sitting on my father's lap on an upholstered chair in a nook between two rooms, stroking his hair.

Unease unfolded in my stomach because something about this scene didn't feel right. Why was my father up so late and why was this strange woman showing him so much affection out here in the open?

"Crystalia, my love, we both have been patient and once Aurora becomes queen you will finally get your magic back. This has been a long process, but in the end it was all worth it," my father said.

My jaw dropped and I stopped breathing for a second. He was with Crystalia—the witch from the forest? Baadar ... his curse ... my father ... the witch. None of this made sense, but a picture was slowly forming...

My father sighed, but he sounded relaxed and happy.

The witch had the firelight and she was immortal, so why would she need me to become queen to get her power back?

"So after all these years, Stefan, was it worth it?" she asked, amusement in her tone. "You managed to get rid of not only your wife but also your daughter, for so long."

I couldn't move. I was rooted to my hiding spot as my heart was jackhammered inside my chest.

Did Crystalia just say that my father was responsible for my curse? And *murdering my mother*? Suddenly, I couldn't breathe.

"Yes, my love. Aurora was a threat to my power. If she found out half the things I did to keep the throne, she'd have ousted me and crowned herself queen a long time ago. That child and her misguided sense of justice..." He sighed and shook his head. "I couldn't leave her be and wait for the hammer to fall. She was never that important to me, anyway. Never truly bonded like father and daughter. I always suspected she wasn't mine, anyway. Leah was quite the whore. I was never certain, not until I killed her mother with my bare hands. Only then did the bitch admit to an affair with a couple of footmen. That woman was foolish. She believed I'd be honorable and spare her life," my father scoffed.

"Even right before her death she was trying to deceive me. She claimed that Aurora was mine, that she was my blood."

The oxygen wasn't getting into my lungs. My blood was drumming in my ears and I felt numb from head to toe. No this couldn't be true. My father couldn't have killed my mother. He'd said she drowned while on a ship years ago. Was this yet another lie? I shouldn't be so surprised...

"I have been without magic for a very long time. The firelight allowed me to use a few spells, but once she becomes queen my own curse will be lifted," Crystalia said and then she leaned over and kissed my father. "I wish there was any other way."

I was too shocked to do anything. They were together and there was a real possibility that I wasn't even his legitimate daughter? My thoughts started racing as memories from the past rushed through my mind. My mother truly loved me, but I finally began to understand why my father was always so distant and cold. All these lies, the pretense, and finally the sleeping curse. It seemed that I had never had a real family.

"My brother must die, no matter what," the king grunted, his voice full of venom and rage.

I hadn't seen him in years but I now realized I never truly knew him. His life had become a dark obsession with vengeance and greed.

"No, I won't let you do it!" I yelled at him, striding out of the shadows and unsheathing my blade. My hands trembled with rage and my heart raced with fury.

Crystalia screamed and leapt out of the king's lap. He looked up at me, his eyes blazing with a fire of hatred.

"Aurora, what are you doing here?" he hissed, his lips curling into a sneer.

"What am I doing here? You made Crystalia curse me years ago with her sleeping spell because you wanted to get rid of me! And you're a fucking murderer, too." Tears sprung to my eyes. to my eyes as I thought of how my poor mother had been taken away from me too soon and without a proper goodbye. "I can't believe you would do this! How could you do something so horrible?"

"I'm sorry, Aurora, but sometimes, drastic measures need to be taken," he said, his voice devoid of emotion.

"And Mother? Did you really kill her?

He didn't respond, but his face darkened as he pursed his lips. "Your mother was never faithful to me and I always doubted you were my daughter," he finally admitted. "I couldn't let you become queen before the curse. That wasn't the right time and I couldn't let a potential bastard child rule over Moorhead."

I wanted to ask the witch about her own curse, but I was running out of time. Crystalia stepped forward, a devious smirk on her face. She raised her hand, index finger pointing at me as she began gathering magic around her. Fireballs crackled in her palm and I began to back away, fear chilling my bones.

"No, my love, you can't kill her just yet. She needs to become the queen." My father bellowed out an ancient incantation and lunged for Crystalia's wrist.

Wait, what? My father had magical powers...

Instantly, the air was filled with an eerie and blinding light, followed by a deafening scream. A wave of flames spread fast across the walls at breakneck speed, traveling to the library, the door of which was open. We all stepped inside but smoke quickly filled the room. As I scrambled back to the exit, I could not breathe and my eyes stung with tears. My father lay motionless on the floor, my blade still clutched in his hand. I didn't remember throwing it, but he must have taken it from me somehow. Too late now. I couldn't get to him on time.

I started to crawl toward him, hoping to drag him out of the library, but my limbs felt like lead and I knew I would not get far enough before being overcome by heat and smoke.

Everywhere around me shimmered with light until all went dark.

"Aurora?" A familiar voice slowly brought me back to the real world. The smoke and fire...

I suddenly felt like I could breathe again. Moments later, I opened my eyes, instantly recognizing my bed and chamber. My whole body felt sore and achy. Phillip was seated beside me, while Baadar stood in the doorway looking more human than I had ever seen him before, deep circles around his eyes, from exhaustion.

"What happened?" I asked, looking at the bandages around my arms. My head hurt when I tried to remember the events that occurred regarding the fire in the library. This definitely wasn't a dream.

Phillip glanced back at Baadar while my heart accelerated. He was here, in the castle, in my chamber, and I was alive. I didn't realize how much I had missed him until now.

"I overheard your exchange with Crystalia and distracted her when she tried to cast her spell, so the whole place lit up in flames. I am not really sure what happened, but the witch caused the explosion that then triggered the fire. You are lucky to be alive, Aurora," Phillip explained, touching my hand.

Then I remembered, and slowly all the memories returned. Baadar, the mating, the barn and the love I felt for him, followed by his betrayal and my departure.

I placed my hands on my head, trying to breathe as I recalled my father and the witch.

"You saved me? How did you even find me?" I asked, my gaze fixed on my king. The one my heart beat for.

He wasn't saying anything at all and I yearned for him to take me in his arms. I needed to feel his warmth. I no longer cared that he was my step-uncle through some twisted design of fate. We were not blood. I never knew him as such. What I knew was that we were always meant to be together.

"It's a long story, but after I realized that Crystalia had used me, we parted ways. She had the firelight, so she didn't need me anymore. I followed her. I managed to track her down on her way to the palace. She was with your father and I couldn't believe that she had been working for him this entire time when I saw them together. I sneaked in the castle, helped by one of the servants loyal to me, and found him outside the library," he explained.

"My father admitted that he was the one that put the sleeping curse on me and he also killed my mother," I whispered, my voice cracking over a sob. The wound inside me was still raw. It was hard for me to grasp that he'd been so utterly evil.

"Your father was many things, Aurora, but he was never a good man," Baadar said, his voice faint.

I wanted him to embrace me, to tell me that he still loved me and everything was going to be fine. I never wanted to be apart from him again.

"Luckily, your father is dead, Aurora. He died with Crystalia in the library when the fire spread. I managed to pull you out before the whole thing collapsed," Phillip admitted and I gasped as I lobbed my gaze from him to Baadar.

"He's gone," I whispered in disbelief. Was I grieving or relieved? I certainly wasn't inclined the man who held no love in his heart for his family.

So now it was all over—the nightmare, the lies, and the ugly magic. Everything had just ended.

"So what now?" I asked, wanting to ask Baadar why he was here and if he'd missed me. I should have been more upset about my father's death, but I couldn't summon much emotion except maybe some regret. He'd schemed to destroy my life and at least, he'd died quickly.

"I will leave you two alone, Aurora. Just don't be too harsh. Baadar is a good man," Phillip said, throwing me a customary wink and leaving the chamber. My body was aching while I stared at the tentacle monster, wondering what the future might bring for both of us.

"You came to check on me?" I asked and then he was beside me, grabbing my hands and kissing them, crying like he couldn't quite believe that I was all right. He was shedding actual tears for me.

"I was so worried about you, my love. I thought you were going to die, you were unconscious for days," he said, kissing my knuckles over and over.

"Look at me, Baadar. Look at me, uncle," I demanded, and he suddenly lifted his head.

"That sounds very dirty coming out of your mouth, my queen," he said, finally sounding like himself.

"We may be related, but I don't care. Deep down we're not blood and fate has brought us together. I missed you and have not stopped loving you," I admitted. "I should have never left with my father."

"You have mated with me and I can't be physically separated from you even if I tried, so I have a proposition for you," he said, smiling.

"I'm listening," I whispered.

"You're going to become Queen of Moorhead and I will step down as king," he said.

I shook my head.

"But you're already King of Moorhead."

"No, I have never been the real ruler of this land. I never wanted the crown. You're the queen and I will become your consort. The kingdom is yours, Aurora," he said, staring at me with such love and determination.

From the looks of it, he'd already made up his mind. I couldn't argue with him anymore though because in my heart of hearts I felt this was the right decision. He was giving up his power for me.

"Consort? You do understand what you're saying," I said. "Are you really going to give up everything, including the crown you've coveted, for me?"

"Yes, my Queen. I want to give you the world and the kingdom doesn't matter as long as you accept me as your consort," he said, moving closer and kissing my lips so gently, so lovingly. Like the beautiful monster he was.

"I accept."

The end

Can't get enough of Aurora and Baadar?
Grab the deleted scene and first chapter of Jane
and the Monster
Click here to get started

Don't forget to follow us on Kickstarter to get
completed story of Jane and Alden

Come hang out with us on Facebook. In our monster
romance group, we talk about anything monster smut
related!
Facebook Smut